Chapter One

Present Day, Early June, Harrison Hall on the James River, Virginia

Lorna Randolph craned her neck at the eighteenth century brick mansion looming above her in the early morning mist. *Holy freaking cow. Like visiting royalty.*

She glanced around the front of the stately home with white columned porches on the first two stories. No sign of a Mrs. Hill, or anyone else. Perhaps she should head indoors. The dewy haze was chilly, and her sweater was in the car.

Flutters danced in her stomach as she clicked up the sandstone steps in her blue strappy sandals. Was she crazy wearing heels for a tour that included the extensive grounds? She badly wanted to succeed in her new job and had upped her usual shorts and t-shirt combo for the intro visit. As long as her heels didn't sink into the damp lawn…

Music? Strains of a vaguely familiar melody reached her from inside the house. A worker with a radio, maybe. Classical stuff. But pretty. Unusual selection for a construction guy.

Where had she heard it before?

Intrigued, and a little intimidated by the imposing structure, she closed her hand around the brass knob on the double front doors and—

1

Zap! A spine-tingling connection jolted through her.

She gasped and stumbled back on the landing. *Where did that come from?*

It wasn't an electrical jolt. She'd been shocked by a faulty outlet before. No. This must stem from another source.

Shaky, but determined, she swung open the door and walked inside. A prickling current ran down her neck, flushing goosebumps over her bare arms and legs.

What the heck? It felt like someone had plugged her in. To what? The house? Even her scalp tingled.

She took a steadying breath and slowly turned, studying the ornate foyer. Sweet-scented beeswax tapers flickered in the brass candelabra on the stand against one ivory wall. A high-backed wooden bench banked another. Queen Anne's lace filled the green Oriental vase on the low table. Framed floral paintings circled the spacious entryway. Everything appeared normal for a colonial manor decorated with period pieces.

Her pale yellow sundress shone in the sparkle of the multifaceted glass chandelier suspended overhead. She'd seen the one-of-a-kind fixture before. But when?

Again, the music summoned her attention. Faint at first, the melodious tune grew more distinct. She dropped her gaze to locate the source of the sound.

A live ensemble? The music seemed to come from a front room, and she detected muffled voices.

Even more unexpected, the chords accompanied laughing dancers forming lines in the entryway. No one told her Harrison Hall had a dance troupe, or that they were performing now, at eight thirty on a Thursday morning. Who drew a crowd at that hour?

Not this group. Someone must've neglected to advertise the event. She, alone, stared at the colorful assembly.

A shame, really. They were totally in character, and looked pure eighteenth century...a painting come to life.

Ladies in flowing silk gowns, like butterfly wings, their hair caught back in cascading curls, and men in formal coats, waistcoats, and knee breeches stepped to the lively melody. Gentlemen swung their partners as men and women came together and whirled away again. Circling, clapping, the couples wove their way down the rows, alternately changing hands with other ladies and gentlemen in the pairing. The floorboards echoed beneath gilt shoes with bows and glittering buckles. Their bright eyes skimmed by her without the slightest acknowledgement.

Strange. She comprised their entire audience. Were they trained to ignore onlookers? They couldn't possibly miss her. She wasn't gonna give a cheesy wave, but she was right here.

The longer she watched them, the more it seemed something was off. Despite their seamless performance, an indefinable quality about the troupe struck her as odd. These were not typical reenactors. Difficult to pinpoint what was different, exactly... They were unarguably genuine, as if carved from time. Isn't this what was wanted?

Doubt nagged.

Holy crap. Depending on how they turned, she could partially see through their forms.

Trick of the light?

The only illumination in the foyer came from the candles, chandelier, and pale sunshine. *Nothing unusual about that.*

Chills crawled down her spine and stood the tiny hairs at the back of her neck on end. The last thing she expected on this June day was a visitation from beyond, and certainly not by merry dancers.

She shrank noiselessly against the wall, pinching her pebbled arms to be certain she was awake.

Could she dream she was pinching herself?

What about the strong scents? The pungency of tobacco smoke and flowery perfumes wafted around her. Were odors a part of dreams? And sounds?

Dear Lord, how was any of this possible?

Uncertain if she were dreaming or haunted, she gaped at the animated figures. *Wait. There. Him.*

Her attention riveted on one young man in the gathering. He'd spun by earlier. She'd swear he gazed over his shoulder in her direction, then promenaded up the hall. His expert steps returned him again to the entryway.

Unlike the other dancers, he was fully corporeal. No partially seen legs or torso. Fitted blue breeches and silk stockings encased his long muscular legs. He wore his own chestnut brown hair pulled back in a queue at his neck, free of powder, while most male heads were wigged and white. The deep blue suit tailored to his tall figure complemented his deft steps in the English country dance.

Something about him held her spellbound…the tilt of his head, arch of his brow, glimpse of his profile… She followed his every move with the fixity of an owl.

He turned blue-gray eyes toward her and sensuous

lips curved into a smile on his handsome face.

Hands down. No contest. He was the hottest guy ever. Her heart beat a thrilling new rhythm.

He circled closer to where she stood rooted in the foyer, not moving a toe, scarcely drawing breath. Did he truly see her backed tremulously against the wall, or did it only feel that way?

Unlike the others in the ghostly assembly, his eyes didn't skirt past her. He paused in the dance. Bending at the shoulders, he tipped his hand to her in a genteel flourish.

He'd freakin' bowed. Her jaw dropped. He most definitely saw her. And she sure as heck saw him.

A sparking sizzle jumped between them, awakening her as she'd never been roused before. Even more than when the house charged through her at her arrival. It was as if she were plugged in—to him.

How that could be, she had no idea, but when he gazed into her eyes, time seemed to stop. She spiraled into moonless stars, and back again to this dizzying realm. To him. Even if she were dreaming, she'd never forget this moment.

"Dance with me." He beckoned to her.

"I don't know how." She forced the panted reply past the tightness in her throat.

He shook his head. "Nae, lady. You are grace itself."

Gallant of him to say. "Clearly, you've never seen me play tennis."

Humor flickered in his eyes and touched his mouth. "I should like to." A look of urgency displaced the fleeting mirth. "Wait. Stay a moment," he entreated.

Was she fading into dreamland, or was he?

Freeing himself from the others, he dashed to her and slipped something into her hand. "Keep this." His voice a whisper in her ear. "I've been waiting for you."

She eyed him incredulously. "But how—"

"Did I know you would be here?" he finished for her, melting tenderness in his gaze. "Because we have been here before." He gestured at the doorway. "Danced through the foyer and into the garden."

"What? When?"

He answered by cupping his hands to her face and pressing his warm lips to hers in a brief, but impassioned kiss. Any remaining breath she had was forfeited to him.

"Until we meet again, sweet lady." He swept her a bow and was gone, and the others with him, like the mist vanishing in the sun streaming through the windows.

She stared after him, or the place he'd been, with her lips slightly parted. There were no words, only her wildly beating heart.

She shook her head to clear it, almost expecting the party—and him—to reappear. No. She was alone in the foyer. It was a dream. He was, too. Had to be. The most vivid, never-to-be-forgotten, dream ever. But she was awake, and when she glanced at her hand, she still held the scrap of paper.

Unfolding it, she mouthed, *Wait for me,* a simple request inked in penmanship that reflected the bold spirit of the young man who'd given it to her.

Her knees were so unsteady she barely kept herself upright. Reason argued with all of her senses. How could she wait for him when she wasn't even certain he was real?

He'd felt divinely real. His presence lingered in the tingles coursing through her, the images dancing in her mind, and the haunting melody she still faintly heard.

Be rational, she chided herself between gasps of air. Where had he and the others come from? *Logically.* If logic entered into this scenario.

Not present-day Virginia.

They must have lived more than two hundred years ago. She couldn't have witnessed them, or him, here now. Or remembered, if that's what this vivid imagery stemmed from.

Despite his assertion to the contrary, she hadn't been to Harrison Hall before, unless her parents brought her here as a child. If so, she didn't recall the visit, and it certainly hadn't been in the eighteenth century. And she'd never been kissed by the sexiest guy on the planet, who claimed a previous acquaintance of the most intimate sort with her. How was such intense familiarity possible?

It wasn't. And yet, she'd seen, heard, felt, and held a scrap of parchment she hadn't clutched when she first entered the house.

What was with this place? The moment she walked through the electrifying door, she'd entered more than an old home. Another world.

Whiffs and glimpses of what must be memories awoke in her. She sniffed the sweetness of jasmine perfume dabbed behind her ears, tasted the luscious chocolate cream dessert spooned from a fluted glass melting on her tongue, waltzed through clipped boxwood hedges in a fragrant moonlit garden...

Wait. She hadn't waltzed there alone. *He'd* circled with her in exhilarating spirals. Who was he?

How did a twenty-first century girl have a barrage of sensations carrying her back to the seventeen hundreds? Had she tumbled into an eighteenth century woman's thought stream? If so, whose? It couldn't be hers.

Could it?

No. She muffled the whispered query.

Perhaps Harrison Hall was a repository for the past, imprinted with glimpses into the lives of those who'd gone before her. Like living, breathing video clips. *Residual ghosts*, she'd heard them called. Or maybe a magnetic field charged with energy had created a paranormal hot spot here.

She probably shouldn't relay these ghostly theories, or her experience, to anyone yet. She couldn't be sure the encounter wasn't just in her head. Whatever the cause of her extraordinary meeting, she was certain of one thing, she had to discover who *he* was.

He mattered, in a deep down, to the core, kind of way. But apart from his being the most unbelievably awesome guy she'd ever met, she couldn't think why. And it seemed to her, that she should, that she'd forgotten something as essential as breathing.

Chapter Two

"Ah, here you are, Miss Randolph. My apologies. I'm running behind this morning."

Lorna jumped at the intrusion into the strange private world she clutched like the precious paper in her hand.

A heavyset woman sailed into the foyer, waving apology. "Sorry if I startled you, honey. I'm Mrs. Hill, tour guide, housekeeper, and all around go-to person."

"That's okay. I figured you were. Pleased to meet you." Her thudding heart made speaking difficult.

"And you." Mrs. Hill looked as if she'd been dropped straight off the streets of colonial Williamsburg. Eighteenth century dress clothed her from the white cap on her head to the snowy apron worn over checked skirts. She must live and breathe this time period.

Despite the knowledgeable woman's fit with the era, Lorna doubted she could be of help in her *unusual* quandary, encompassing all of: 'what just happened to me,' nor was she about to ask.

After four harsh years of high school, and a traitorous best friend making out with her cheater ex-boyfriend, she'd been ecstatic to land a summer job at Harrison Hall. Sure beat working in fast food while she saved for community college, paid better, and offered an escape from all the drama. A crash course in colonial homes, via touring as many old manors as she and her mom could cram into the week after graduation, gave her a clue about historic houses.

Even with her advance prepping, she suspected the current owner, Mr. Cable, must be desperate to take on such a youthful novice. She'd been hired after a mere phone interview with Mrs. Hill and a few emails from him. But her mom, and consequently she, could claim kin to his aunt's late husband, Walter Randolph, which might account for the quick hire. Kin are kin in the South, no matter how distant the ties, and the Randolph's were tied to Harrison Hall. With Mr. Cable in a hurry to take on a new trainee, she wasn't gonna argue her good fortune.

No explanation given. None required. *Right*?

Mrs. Hill halted in a flurry of skirts, her pale blue eyes welcoming. "Have you met any of the others yet?"

"No, ma'am." Apart from her recent visitors, that is, and Lorna wasn't saying a word about them. It was all she could do to answer straightforward questions.

The woman's round face creased in affection. "You'll like everyone. Mr. Cable lives here with his elderly aunt and some of the staff. You're to stay, too, I understand."

"Yes. He generously offered me room and board. A relief to my mom who feared where on earth I'd live."

"Glad that worked out for you. We best get a move on, gal. The house opens at ten. Visitors traipse through until four, and someone—chiefly me—has to conduct the tours." She scuttled ahead like a fluffed up hen in her layers of cloth. "I'll show you the rooms, then turn you over to Mr. Hodge, our head gardener, for a grounds tour."

"Right. Coming." Lorna jerked to life, part of her reluctant to leave the spot where *he'd* been. No good having the welcoming committee think she was high on day one. She wasn't that sort of teen, just one who seemingly communed with the past, in a passionately personal kind of way.

She hastened after Mrs. Hill's disappearing skirts and passed through an ivory archway leading to the rest of the house. The blue, purple, and gold carpet running up the hall muted her heels. 'Follow the yellow brick road.' Or near enough. She may well have landed in *Oz*.

Breathless from excitement and her dash after the surprisingly fast guide, she caught up with her in the parlor, or one of them. There might be several in this large home.

"Note the craftsmanship." The enthusiast waved at their elegant surroundings, her linen sleeve sliding back over a plump freckled arm.

"This is where the family entertains special guests and holds dances, that sort of thing. Been that way since the house was built. Not many grand affairs these days but there's a ball planned for midsummer, same as the summer solstice. Less than three weeks away, and much to do."

She gestured at the harpsichord in the corner. "That was a gift to the Harrison family from George Washington himself. Cost a heap to have it repaired. Plays real nice now. Mr. Cable is overseeing the improvements to the house and grounds after the place got to be too much for his aunt. Wants everything ready for Lady Jane's 90th—" She broke off, and her face flushed. "That's what we call Mrs. Randolph, only not to her face. She's a good sort, just a bit peculiar."

By 'we,' Lorna assumed Mrs. Hill meant herself and the other employees. Come to think of it, her mother had mentioned the elderly woman's eccentricities. Maybe Mrs. Randolph fancied herself aristocracy. Heck, maybe she was.

She laid a hand on the housekeeper's well-padded shoulder. "Your secret's safe with me." And she didn't dare spill her own.

Approval in her eyes, Mrs. Hill nodded at the two fiddles in cases on a high-legged table. "Valuable instruments." She waved at the sheets of paper covered in musical notes. A quilled pen and ink pot appeared in recent use, as did the nearby stool. Shaking her capped head, she clucked at the untidiness. "Mr. Cable's composing again. Good thing this room's cordoned off so visitors don't get too close. Someone would upset that ink."

This explained the tasseled cord forming a perimeter around much of the parlor.

"Ah well." She smiled indulgently. "He's a genius. Even composes some pieces in the old style, as you can see. But he's got electronic equipment for that upstairs in his study."

More chills, like scattering ants, flushed down Lorna's spine. The melody she'd heard in the entryway was played on a harpsichord and stringed instruments. *These, maybe*? And the scrap in her hand might have come from the page missing a corner, and the ink from the blue flowered china pot.

'Curiouser and curiouser.' For once, *Alice in Wonderland* made more sense than her real life.

Her heart drummed so loudly she thought the

talkative woman must hear the pounding over her chatter. Maybe she should run while she still could. If she fled the house, the pleasant-faced guide would wonder. Besides, she was too intrigued by the mystery man to bolt.

What was that? Faint music emanated from the very walls. A beautiful, haunting tune. Not the dance melody from before. Different. Did Harrison Hall have its own soundtrack?

Unlikely.

Maybe the song was in her head? Mrs. Hill retained her placid expression.

Perhaps she was unaware. Maybe the house had a message for Lorna, and Lorna alone. The thought sent tremors prickling through her. She must appear racked with cold.

The effusive guide didn't seem to notice. Rather, she gazed around her with pride. "Isn't the parlor lovely? And freshly painted in the original colors."

So shaky she expected the floor to claim her at any moment, Lorna took in the spacious—by colonial standards—pale blue room. "Very nice."

Her gratified companion pointed at the high ivory ceiling. "Those plaster cornices in the upper corners are designed with geometric motifs and sculpted molding that display skills from long-dead craftsmen. Restored to the original."

Impressive. *But crap.* She'd just been kissed by a hot guy original to this era.

"Look there. In the light." A plump finger directed her attention to the window and couch. The gracefully arched gold sofa shone in the buttery stream flowing beneath the blue valance at the window. An orange tabby snoozed on a couch cushion in the sunbeams.

"Sweet." She followed the woman's insistent digit to the wood nymphs and green vines festooning the frieze above the marble fireplace.

"All restored," the devotee assured her.

The mural triggered a chord inside Lorna. "Charming," she managed, with the eerie sensation she'd seen this before.

"Isn't it?" Her smiling guide motioned at the two crimson armchairs before the hearth. "Georgian style." She waved at the high-backed upholstered chairs lining the far wall. "Queen Anne," she preened. "The small tables interspersed throughout the room are occasional tables, used for various purposes."

"I see." But Lorna already knew.

The voluptuous fragrance of roses drew her focus to the pink flowers in the floral vase on the mantel. The old-fashioned blossoms were bunchy like peonies, but their season had ended and roses were in bloom. A few satiny petals drifted beside the porcelain figurines on either side of the arrangement. A curly-haired girl in frills hugged a white lamb. Another girl herded a mama duck and ducklings. An assortment of china dogs kept them company.

"Those pieces are Staffordshire and two hundred and fifty years old. Harrison Hall has a long tradition of fondness for animals," Mrs. Hill remarked.

Lorna remembered, or was beginning to.

The housekeeper gave the kitty an affectionate pat, purrs rumbling in response. "Lady Jane—I mean Mrs. Randolph—is devoted to Jasper here. The official house cat. Mr. Cable has a Siamese, Lyle." She eyed Lorna quizzically. "You like cats?"

"Love them." She'd reluctantly left two cats with her mom and younger sisters. Her father often traveled with his job and was indifferent to the number of felines they acquired, as long as they kept them under half a dozen.

Everywhere her gaze wandered, she spotted weirdly familiar furnishings and touches. A cabinet stuffed with china pieces held a regal couple curtsying and bowing for all eternity. She'd swear she'd seen them before, and the musical accompaniment was like a haunting theme song.

The child's miniature tea set decorated with purple violets against a green background drew her eye. She envisioned a fair-haired girl seated on a blanket in the garden having a tea party with the tiny cups and teapot.

For someone who'd never been here, she sure recognized a lot of things. With no explanation she cared to accept, she just went with the uncanny flow. "Wonderful room, Mrs. Hill, but is it large enough for a ball?"

"Depends on how many attend. If it gets too crowded, the dancers spread throughout the house. Even into the entryway."

"Of course." She nodded at the consuming memory.

A buzzing halted the animated woman. She reached into a hidden pocket and withdrew a cell phone. How out-of-place the modern device looked in the eighteenth century world Lorna had entered. Her own phone, set to mute, rode in the small purse hanging by a thin strap over her shoulder. She'd texted her arrival first thing, and nothing since. What could she say?

Mrs. Hill frowned beneath the white cap Lorna hoped she wouldn't have to wear. She tucked several graying auburn curls into place and glanced up. "They're out of lavender oil in the shop. You know, the one Mr. Cable set up on the grounds? Anyway, I've got to make a run to the lavender farm for more."

"That's fine. We can finish the tour later."

"Humph," the perturbed guide grunted. "Not much later left in the day. Tell you what; show yourself around as best you can. Don't forget the gardens, and help yourself to refreshments in the kitchen." She eyed her in concern. "You've gone a bit pale. Don't want you fainting from low blood sugar. Tell Cook Betty I sent you." With that thoughtful addition, she bustled off as a matron with a busy household might have done in bygone days.

Not so bygone now.

Bewildered beyond words, Lorna sank onto the couch beside the cat and slid her purse to the upholstery. Whether it was low blood sugar, hallucinations, or such desperation for a boyfriend that she'd created one, she didn't know. Nor how to account for the 'memories.'

Her mom and sisters would be engrossed by her account. She was too mystified to know where to begin. Watching *Ghost Hunters* was one thing, living it quite another. And this was far more.

Glad for some quiet, she huddled with the purring kitty. His contentment soothed her. She'd had a late night packing and an early start to her increasingly strange day. Normally, she was described as energetic. Overwhelmed and unaccountably fatigued better suited her current state.

The room lulled her frazzled mind. Sorting her jumbled thoughts was beyond her, like trying to solve a convoluted whodunit without enough of the clues. Better to soak in the peace. A robin sang beyond the window, and bees droned in the white hydrangea blossoms below the sill, as they would have centuries ago…

How many moments passed, she wasn't certain. She must've dozed off, because the next thing she knew, someone gently nudged her shoulder. "Tea?" a low voice asked.

She blinked and glanced around drowsily. A young man in a brown and green-faced uniform with pewter buttons bent near her and held out a steaming china cup. Her gaze traveled down buff-colored breeches fitted to his long legs. He wore polished black riding boots.

An American Revolutionary War reenactor? She took the cup, and their eyes met. She sucked in her breath. "You."

He nodded. "Me."

Like a stream overflowing its banks, a surge of emotions rushed through her. Shaking hands betrayed her volatile reaction.

He covered her trembling fingers with his warm grasp, steadying the cup. "Have care. It's hot."

Only a vague awareness of the near mishap penetrated her astonishment. His tantalizing presence made her falter, yet want to plunge ahead in the same gulp. At first, no words escaped her. Then she blurted, "But before, at the dance, you were in civilian clothes."

Somber lines etched his good looks. "That was then. This is now."

"It wasn't more than an hour ago," she stammered, not certain if she argued with a man or ghost.

He arched chestnut brows. "Time must pass rather differently for you. It's been two years since that meeting."

The grandfather clock in the hall chimed nine thirty. "The clock begs to differ."

"What does it truly know of time?" He sighed, lowering himself beside her, and the irate cat stalked off. A faint smile returned to his appealing mouth. "See what I've done? Annoyed his highness. Please, drink your tea, Miss Randolph. You've had quite a shock."

"You can say that again."

He furrowed his brow. "What would be the point?"

"What, indeed? It's a stupid saying." She sipped dazedly from the flowered porcelain. The strong sweetened brew strengthened her, and she collected herself to face him. "I want the man back who I met before."

His mouth tightened, then opened. "He's a hardened soldier now, fighting a war against the British Empire he may lose."

"You won't. Lose, I mean."

Again, the faint smile. "That is most welcome news. You can foretell the future?"

She shook her head. "I am the future."

"Ah. I see." Sadness touched eyes the hue of the sky before a rain. He lifted his hand, slipping a strand of her shoulder length blonde hair between his fingers. A shiver rippled through her. "That must make me the past," he said huskily. "And I so want to share the present with you."

"Perhaps we can meet in the middle?" Though she

had no earthly clue how.

"Perhaps." He tilted his head to one side considering her. A soft light suffused his gaze. "You waited for me?"

She took the paper from her lap and held it out. "A whole hour."

He chuckled. "Time is notably different for you. Your faithfulness is admirable nonetheless."

She drank him in, his every look and gesture. He smelled of soap, leather, and his own masculine essence. "For you, kind sir, I would wait more than an hour. But I don't even know your name."

"Do you not?" He brushed calloused fingers roughened from riding over her cheek and sent more shivers through her. "Forgive me, dear lady. I am Lieutenant Hart Harrison, and Harrison Hall is my family home."

Goosebumps pebbled her from head-to-toe. "What is the year, Lieutenant Harrison?"

"Seventeen seventy-seven, and please, call me Hart. Few do these days."

"Very well. Dear Hart, whom I've only just met but feel I've known for years, am I in your world or are you in mine?"

"Is there a difference?"

Tiny quivers scattered through her. "More than two centuries. Last time I checked, the year was twenty seventeen."

He absorbed this mindboggling disclosure for a long moment. If she expected protest, denial, or disbelief, she received none. He remained intent on her, his manner earnest.

"You have journeyed quite a distance," he simply

said.

"So it would seem. But I didn't go anywhere except here, to your home."

"Are you content to stay?"

"I am hired to work here this summer."

"A lady of your standing, hired for pay?" He couldn't have looked more shocked if she'd stated she was a whore.

"Nothing indecent," she hastened to amend. "Only to work in the house and grounds."

"Such work is not suited for the fair Lady Lorna Randolph."

How impressive he made her sound, as if she'd stepped from a carriage in a royal robe. "It's a grand title. Still, I assure you I am in want of funds."

"Stay here with me and I will care for you."

Old-fashioned but sweet of him. "How? You're at war."

"My mother and sister remain at the house. Father serves under General Washington. The women will be glad of your charming company, and I will visit as I'm able." His eyes caressed her. "We were to be betrothed, before I rode off to war."

"We were?" She cast her mind back. Not in her lifetime. Had she shared a former one with him? "How do you know my name?"

He smiled slightly. "I've known you since you were a wee lass pouring tea for your dollies. But you slipped away from me." Moisture glistened in his eyes. "At long last, I've found you again."

She remembered the child's tea set and struggled to comprehend the unfathomable. "Slipped away? How?"

He shook his head. "Makes no difference now."

"But it does." His liquid gaze said as much.

"Nae." He brushed aside her insistence. "Your attire is different, and your hair shorter than the woman I knew, but you are still you. Stay, Lorna."

"Have I a choice?" She didn't remember leaving him before.

"Always." Lowering his head, he pressed his lips to hers and covered her mouth in a searing kiss.

Drums pounded in her chest, and fire inflamed her. He enfolded her in his strong arms, holding her to his muscular chest, and she lost herself in him. If this were a most peculiar and delicious dream, and she awoke, she'd be desolate. But how could it be anything else?

God help her, she prayed he was real.

Chapter Three

Let this moment go on and on. Lorna's petition rose on rapturous wings, while outside the parlor window a robin serenaded the couple from the magnolia tree.

Never in the history of mankind had there been such a kiss. Not even in *The Princess Bride*. She sensed this sacred moment was several centuries in the making, and she still didn't know if Hart were made of flesh and blood.

He must be. A ghost couldn't feel like this.

Could he?

No. Lorna was no expert on spirts from beyond. She didn't need one to see Hart Harrison was more vibrantly alive than anyone she'd ever known. And yet, their being together wasn't possible. Part of her wanted to stay forever, and the other to bolt from the rabbit hole while she still could.

Nix that. It was already too late. She was indelibly bound to him, and didn't even know why.

Nothing made any sense. Not remotely. But she wasn't a flighty bunny. Whatever it took. She'd stay. She'd discover.

Profoundly perplexed, she parted from his captivating lips. "How?" The breathy word escaped her.

He traced the tip of his finger over her mouth. "Divine Providence has returned you to me."

There it was again. The implication that she'd gone. "Where did I go? The future?"

"It would seem thus."

As before, he'd left much unsaid.

"I would wipe the bewilderment from your eyes," he whispered. "The shade of blue forget-me-nots that bloom in the spring garden." He slid a gold locket from his waistcoat pocket and opened it. "See."

A miniature portrait of a girl about Lorna's age gazed back at her, and nearly stopped her hammering heart. "Dear God. She looks just like me."

"She's Miss Lorna Randolph." A huskiness deepened his low voice.

"Are there two of us? What happened? Tell me."

He considered her in wash of tenderness. "You have no memory of our pact?"

She strove to think back, combing the distant echoes of her mind. "None. Yet somewhere inside me, I know you."

"Yes. Since childhood."

"Not the childhood I recently experienced," she argued.

He restored the locket. "The one vague to your memory, then. You spent years here with my family."

The increasingly familiar prickles darted through her. She must be one ginormous goosebump. "You speak as if we grew up together."

"We did."

"How?" She gulped. "Why? Are we kin?" *Please Lord, don't let them be cousins.*

"No. My family took you in after your parents died of fever."

In that moment, she experienced the expression

'someone walking over her grave' as a shiver... The feeling occurred forcefully to her.

Do you feel expressions?

She did, and if she weren't quite certain her present-day mom and dad were all right, she'd have dropped over. "This is why you invited me to stay in your home with your family?"

"That, and the understanding between us."

Again, the insistence they were engaged. She waved at the elegant room dappled in morning light. "I'm here and don't see a soul, unless they're elsewhere."

"They are," he assured her. "Do you think for an instant I would abandon all decorum and pay intimate attentions to you if my mother and sister, or anyone else, looked on?"

"No. You are far too mannerly for that."

A smile tugged at his lips. "Thank you for noting."

"Still, I suspect your family might not be able to see me even if they did observe us," she mused aloud. "The other dancers didn't."

He gazed fully at her. "You were a heavenly beam to them. Glowing like an angel, wreathed in golden light."

Her face heated at his compliment, and her head swirled under the force of his eyes. "The chandelier caught my yellow dress and hair. And the sun was breaking through."

He shook his head. "Nae. 'Twas night."

Breath escaped her in a whoosh. "Holy freaking cow."

The corners of his eyes crinkled. "What is holy about a *freaking* cow?"

"Nothing. It's just an expression of amazement. Kind of lame." She stared at him. "We don't even share the same time of day, let alone year, or century. Is it possible, you're a long lost *Time Lord*?" She hadn't thought they were real.

His smile radiated through her. "No lordship to my knowledge. I'm an officer and a gentleman. Perhaps, it is you who are mistress of time."

"Perhaps. And maybe there's truth to the *Doctor Who* assertion that time is 'more like a big ball of wibbly-wobbly, timey-wimey…stuff,' rather than strictly linear, as we perceive it."

He arched chestnut-colored brows. "I'm not even going to inquire about this strange doctor and his theory." He entwined his fingers with hers. "Whatever the cause of our reunion, sweet lady, you are with me. Wonderfully corporeal to my touch."

"As are you. But if I venture from this room, will I return to find you a wizened old man?"

A low chuckle escaped him. "I think not."

"Yet you tell me two years have passed, and I've only journeyed from the entryway to the parlor. Our two worlds are co-mingling, and us with them." She flushed. "I didn't mean that the way it sounded."

He raised both hands in mock surrender. "I make no protest if you did."

She clasped his broad shoulders. "But don't you see? We may have little control over how events play out."

Solemnity displaced his humor. "You are correct. We cannot. Only promise to seek the other. Always. Will you swear to this?"

Lost in him, she crossed her heart. "Yes. I swear."

The hall clock struck ten. "Oh my." She clapped a hand to her forehead. "I'm supposed to tour the house and grounds in preparation for my duties here. My guide, the housekeeper, Mrs. Hill, had to leave."

"Pray, allow me the honor of conducting the tour. While I disapprove of you lifting a finger in manual labor, who better to guide you through Harrison Hall than its heir?"

"No one, I suppose. Yet, for you, the future is my past. Well, the house's past, really," she faltered, aware she was blathering. "I'm only eighteen."

"And I'm barely three years your senior."

"Actually, you're more than two hundred years older, but who's counting?"

The faintest smile touched his lips. "Let us take life as we find it."

"Agreed. I have no idea how else to take it. The realm I've entered is too incredible for words."

"For me, also. Well then, Miss Randolph, allow me to assist you to your feet." He rose, drawing her up with him, and the scrap of paper fluttered to the floor. He bent to retrieve the note and tucked it into his waistcoat pocket beside the locket. He extended his arm. "Shall we proceed?"

"Yes. Let's."

She hooked her arm through his and walked across the parlor at his side. Her head reached just below his shoulder. But she wondered, when they stepped through that door, would it be into her world or his?

****

"I'm back, Miss Randolph. A gal from the lavender farm was making deliveries and met me halfway." Mrs. Hill's blowsy skirts and reddened face greeted Lorna and Hart in the hall outside the parlor. She must have one speed. Hyperdrive.

Halting before them, she tilted her head at the newcomer in the manner of an inquisitive bird. She blotted her beaded forehead and round cheeks with a linen handkerchief smelling sweetly of lavender and surveyed the man at Lorna's side. A gleam of approval lit her pale blue eyes.

No surprise there, and no need for Lorna to introduce the absorbed woman to Hart; he must know this was the housekeeper she'd mentioned.

Mrs. Hill fluttered the square cloth at him. "Well, well. Mr. Cable has taken on a new reenactor, has he? Never said a word to me. He's outdone himself, this time. My, you do look the part. Ride with the *Virginia Horse* do you, soldier?"

He inclined his head. "Yes, ma'am. The 1st Continental Regiment of Light Dragoons under command of Colonel Bland."

"Distinguished company. *Bland's Horse,* I believe you're called. Excellent riders. Best in the Continental Army, I've heard, though I do speak as a fellow Virginian."

He colored slightly. "High praise, madame. I thank you. How is it you are acquainted with the regiment?"

"I've worked as a costume mistress for historical productions." Her appreciative gaze swept him from head-to-boot. "I see you're wearing the earlier brown and green-faced uniform before the regiment switched to the blue and red-faced variety. Now *that* was an eye-catching uniform. What year are you portraying?"

If her keen interest discomfited him, he didn't let on, and maintained his composure. "The year of Our

Lord seventeen hundred and seventy-seven."

"Ah." She grimaced. "Bad year for the Continental Army. Though Washington won earlier at Trenton and Princeton."

"Yes, ma'am. Quite a feat," he agreed, probably wondering what was next on the battle agenda. "The general is unmatched in courage and wits. Unfortunately, we lack the forces to hold the field and must promptly withdraw."

She gave a sage nod. "Getting men and keeping them was always a struggle. If reenactors of today had to face what those troops endured, they'd be few and far between."

The slight furrow at his brow indicated he was a bit puzzled. Probably more than a bit. "You are, indeed, acquainted with the state of affairs, ma'am."

"Oh, yes. I'm a fan of all things colonial and the American Revolution ranks high on my list of favorites."

This exchange could last awhile, and Lorna wanted Hart to herself. She cleared her throat. "Lieutenant Harrison has offered to show me around the house and grounds."

Mrs. Hill jerked to attention. "Good heavens above. That explains why you look so familiar. You're the image of Hart Harrison. His portrait is in the downstairs bedroom on display for visitors. I didn't realize Mr. Cable was having a reenactor play the part of the early owner of Harrison Hall. What a splendid idea," she rushed on, not pausing for breath. "You're familiar with the place, are you?"

"Since boyhood."

Her ruddy face curved in a grin. "Wonderful old

home. And I like to think we've maintained, even expanded, the gardens. Did your parents bring you here as a child?"

"They are responsible for my acquaintance with Harrison Hall, yes. I echo your sentiments regarding its beauty."

She bobbed her capped head. "Well then, it would be a big help to have you show Miss Randolph around."

The color in his cheeks heightened, and he gave a low bow. "I should be delighted."

Beaming up at him as if he were the answer to her prayers, she continued. "How long will you be with us?"

The gray hue in his blue gaze deepened. "I am not certain. Duty bids my return to the regiment before long. The colonel depends on me."

Lead weighted Lorna's gut. She supposed being from the past and an already completed era didn't excuse him from returning to this point in his life cycle. Though, more and more, she wished it did.

Mrs. Hill eyed him with respect, her mouth parted. "My, you really stay in character. I'm better at gauging uniforms than I am at keeping all the battles straight. Big one on the horizon, is there, Lieutenant?"

"Battle is inevitable. But I have received no official word from couriers."

"If a courier arrives on horseback, I'll send him to you immediately," she promised with a wink.

"Pray do."

She nodded briskly. "The only big upcoming battle I'm aware of is Brandywine in Pennsylvania in September."

He shifted in his black boots. "If I didn't believe

you to be a Patriot, ma'am, I should wonder at your being a British spy."

A smile curved her lips at the supposed compliment. "That battle is marked by annual ceremonies and events. What is General Washington doing this fine summer of seventeen seventy-seven?"

Hart explored her with the unwavering regard of a cat. "Perhaps you should tell me."

She giggled. "No, really. I can't recall."

"Skirmishing with General Howe's forces in New Jersey, last I heard."

"Right. In seventy-seven, Howe hasn't yet been replaced by General Clinton as the British Commander-in-Chief to America."

Was she testing him?

The furrow at his brow deepened. "No, though it's good to hear General Howe botches his campaign."

Her eyes sparkled. "Not entirely but enough to be sent packing. You have such a detailed grasp of events, as if you're actually fighting in the war."

His somberness made a stark contrast to her enthusiasm. "I am, madame. Sickness takes a greater toll on troop numbers than injury and death from combat." Scorn crossed his gaze. "And desertion thins the ranks."

"So I've heard. Pity, that." She patted his arm. "You certainly know your stuff and possess such an impressive presence. A truly magnificent portrayal. Are you staying nearby, or does Mr. Cable have you bunking at the house?"

Hart exchanged glances with Lorna. "In truth, madame, I am not aware of my accommodations. If need be, I can bed down in the stable with my mount. I am hardened to camp life."

She made a shooing gesture. "I wouldn't hear of it. I will consult with Mr. Cable and see what he has in mind. Now, you two had best be off, if you're to complete your tour before lunch. The staff eat in the kitchen at twelve thirty."

He offered another short bow. "Until then." With Lorna hanging on his arm, he turned away and escorted her down the hall, out of earshot.

The continual impression of being in a dream accompanied her. "We're still in my world, Hart."

"For now."

"You make a fabulous couple," Mrs. Hill called after them. "We'll get Miss Randolph properly attired later today. Perhaps, she could play the part of the ward of the Harrison family and—" She broke off. "My word. I just realized. She has the same name as that girl. What a coincidence."

"Isn't it just." Lorna couldn't begin to take it all in.

"Wondrous, Mrs. Hill." Hart paused and turned them both back around. "But then, Miss Randolph descends from the early Randolph family. I believe you will discover she bears a striking resemblance to the original Lorna Randolph in her portrait."

"Good heavens." Mrs. Hill was slack-jawed. She swiveled her stare at Lorna, all the while mopping her florid face. "Funny I didn't notice sooner. Must be her hair and clothes being so different. You're right, though, her face is the spitting image of the young lady in the painting."

"Where is it?" Lorna whispered to him.

He nodded at the closed door across from the parlor. "In the dining room, if it's still there."

"Must be, as excited as Mrs. Hill is."

She advanced on them, waving her hands in the air, and the handkerchief like a flag. But this formidable woman wasn't surrendering. More likely, she was preparing to charge.

"Great God in heaven. We must take advantage of this rare opportunity. Two young people who look like the originals from the Revolutionary War era of this house? And it's rumored they were to wed. Such a tragic romance. Think of the publicity. The crowds we could draw. They're thin on the grounds this morning, I can tell you. But the pair of you could revive interest and bring in revenue for improvements and upkeep. It's a miracle. I must talk to Mr. Cable and Lady Jane—I mean, Mrs. Randolph."

What the freaking heck? Lorna opened and closed her mouth. No words came out. What if Hart disappeared in the middle of whatever performance they were expected to enact? What if she vanished with him? And why was their story tragic?

Not sharing the housekeeper's jubilation, he stood rigid beside Lorna. "What of our tour?"

She waved him aside. "That can wait," she insisted, seizing his arm, as though she feared he'd get away. And he just might. "Let's go and find Mr. Cable. Chances like this happen only once in a lifetime. If that."

Unless Lorna was lost in a dream, she had two lifetimes to contend with and little memory of what happened in the former one. The sense that these lives were connected both frightened and thrilled her. She and Hart were living history. Mrs. Hill didn't begin to grasp how much.

Would Mr. Cable have a clue? If so, what might he do?

She and Hart must remain together. This was crucial. They had a mystery to solve, and scant time to do it. She felt it in her very bones. A glance at his somber expression told her he knew even more than she did.

But what? She could hardly ask now. Admittedly, part of her didn't want to learn the answers.

"Come on. Mr. Cable's in his study at the top of the stairs." Petticoats swishing, Mrs. Hill charged ahead.

"The woman could command troops," he said under his breath and gestured at Lorna. "After you, fair lady."

With him behind her, she followed Mrs. Hill up the winding staircase to meet the current owner of Harrison Hall. Would spirits of the past shadow their steps?

She shivered in the air-conditioning, so out of place in this eighteenth century manor, though she understood it must be temperature controlled to preserve the artifacts. Odd to consider, Hart was one of them. Apparently, in a weird way, so was she.

"You grow chilled. Here." He gently folded the coat of his uniform around her bare shoulders.

The heavy linen hung nearly to her knees but she appreciated his thoughtfulness. She reached back to brush his hand, and he took her fingers firmly in his grasp. This much was real.

"My mother awaits us on the landing," he whispered.

What? Lorna lifted her gaze to the woman in a green gown and brown hair dressed high on her head beneath a small lace cap. Surprise widened eyes the same blue-gray as Hart's. There was a familiar quality about her.

Where on earth had Mrs. Hill gone? The dynamic woman had disappeared, while the presumed Mrs. Harrison held out welcoming arms, her flounced sleeves fluttering with lace. "Hart, you're home in time for Adelaide's birthday."

She shifted her focus to Lorna, who must appear extremely odd in her modern attire, draped in his coat. The puzzled woman squinted at the newcomer by candlelight, her eyes widening in stark disbelief. "Can this be our Lorna?"

Chapter Four

Silent as the grave, Lorna stared back into Mrs. Harrison's incredulous gaze. *What the heck?*

How had she and Hart gone from following Mrs. Hill up the steps in twenty seventeen to the eighteenth century, in the space of an instant? If this was his mother, then that's where they were. No denying they'd shot back in time.

The woman went white.

"Hold on, Mama." He propelled Lorna forward by the elbow and sped them both to the landing. Snaking out a strong arm, he wrapped it around his slender, still pretty mother. His swift action prevented her from slumping to the hard floorboards

She rolled frightened eyes at him. "How can this be? Did we not bury the dear girl?"

I'm dead? Technically, Lorna realized someone from the seventeen hundreds must be long gone, but *Dear God.* Had she bridged the centuries only to learn of her untimely demise?

No need to worry about there being two of her in the same era. No meeting her past self and all of that *Back to the Future* warning stuff. Not a chance. But dead? And no memory of it? *Holy freakin' moly.* She defined creepola.

Weakness assailed her knees, and Hart threw his free arm around her shoulder. An awkward group hug ensued with the two of them clutched in his embrace. "Let's get you both to the parlor." Emotion roughened his voice.

Annoyance flashed in Lorna alongside her numbing shock. "You might have given me a heads-up on the whole dying thing," she hissed near his ear. This must be how she'd slipped away from him in the first place.

"Not the time," he attempted.

"Seriously?" Anger emboldened her flagging spirits, while his poor mother seemed on the verge of a faint.

Not quite.

A low wail issued from between her pale lips. "'Tisn't natural, arising from the grave. What foul creature has assumed dear Lorna's shape?"

"Great going, Hart," Lorna bit out. "Now, she thinks I'm a zombie."

He turned his head at her. "A what?"

"*The Walking Dead.*" He didn't need to see the television show to get the general meaning of the term. Not particularly flattering.

She disengaged herself from his support and left him to uphold his rapidly disintegrating mother. "How am I supposed to be *charming company,* as you termed it, to your family, if they think I'm deceased?"

Exasperation flared in his wounded gaze. "Plainly, you're not dead."

"And plainly, you haven't thought this through." She waved her hand at the upstairs hall, flagged with candelabras and family portraits stretching down a long corridor. "I am *here,* in this realm. You might have mentioned I'm supposed to be in my grave."

His dazed parent roused from her near stupor. "God forgive me, did I entomb the poor girl alive?"

Had Mrs. Harrison been in charge of her burial?

"No, Mama," He assured her.

Another wail escaped the distraught female. "Then how is it she stands before me?"

This wasn't going well.

Horror twisted her face into a stricken mask. "Perhaps she roused in her coffin and called out. Some passerby must have unearthed the piteous child, and she's wandered ever since, driven mad by her terrible trial."

He patted her shoulder. "No. No. She's not mad."

His mother fluttered her fingers at the supposed deceased from beneath the lace flounced sleeve. "But her hair, her manner of dress. Her ankles show and her shoes have no toes." Another gasping wail. "Dear Lord above and all the holy angels. She's clawed her way from the grave and fallen into harlotry."

"Hardly that," Lorna protested. "And this happens to be my best sundress." To think she'd agonized over wearing these strappy sandals because of the heels.

The frightened woman didn't reply. She drooped unheeding against Hart.

Lorna shot him a reproachful glance. "Where were you when they lowered me into the cold ground?"

"On it, off fighting for freedom from tyranny." Pain welled in his eyes. "News of your death destroyed me. I was utterly incapacitated. No man could route me from my tent. The threat of dismissal availed nothing. I would have faced the British Legion without a care. And then…" he trailed off.

"Oh, no," she pounced. "Don't pull that again. Tell

me."

He met her insistence through the liquid film glinting in his gaze. "You appeared to me, as clearly as you are now, and promised we would be together again."

"I did? Why can't I remember any of this?"

He shrugged, the wonder in his face a reflection of the awe stirring in her heart. "At first, I thought you a dream or a spirit, but you were real. I felt your arms around me." A hint of bliss transformed his expression. "You urged me not to give up and to fight on. Your sweet presence kindled fresh hope, and I was renewed."

"That's how you knew you'd find me?"

His gaze promised a wealth of togetherness. "I have never given up on that promise. Fever took you from me, but it could not steal you forever."

Tiny chills rippled through her and sent prickles over her arms. "When you saw me at the dance, was I already—"

"Departed? Yes."

Amazement made speech a challenge. "So I was a ghost?"

"Nae." His entire being seemed to entreat her to believe. "Your appearance was ethereal, not ghostly. And I soon saw you were made of flesh and blood."

"I prefer angelic to an apparition. But why were you not wearing your uniform then?"

"In seventeen seventy-five, I did not yet have this one. We wore what passed for regimental dress in the field. The night I attended the dinner and dance at Harrison Hall was to please Mama." He glanced down at the woman, apparently in a swoon. "She was desperate to push the war away, so I wore fashionable attire. When I spotted you, my heart leapt for joy. You kept your promise, even if you forgot the reason, then you began to fade."

"Me? No. You did. To mist."

Another shrug, and warmth charged his expression. "However we parted, I continued to seek you with confidence. Today, I was rewarded beyond my deepest hopes."

"All your days and years of seeking are but hours for me. Didn't you wonder at my still wearing the same dress?"

"A little. Yet if I am prepared to embrace your return, why trifle over a gown?"

"Good point." She gazed at him, trying to comprehend the incomprehensible. "And now we're together? In what, the present or the past, or both?"

A moan from the prostrate female returned their attention to the present, which weirdly, was the past.

"Let us attend to her." He strode ahead, bearing his mother in his arms.

Uncertain of anything except Hart, Lorna followed him into the upstairs parlor. Likely, this was the same room they were supposed to be seated in right now meeting with Mr. Cable. What must he and Mrs. Hill think of their sudden departure, assuming the housekeeper had alerted her employer?

The woodsy scent and sight of the crackling fire lent a homey atmosphere to the unreal scene. Mrs. Harrison roused slightly as Hart gently settled her in the gold upholstered chair before the warming hearth. He tucked the shawl draped on the back of the chair around her thin shoulders.

The coolness in the house was unexpected. They

had no air-conditioning in the eighteenth century. "Is it June here, too?"

"Yes." He glanced at the darkened window, spattered by rain. "But not morning. The gloom suggests a cloudy evening."

"Why are days and nights mixed up in this time travel conundrum?"

"To answer that, we need a formidable wizard." He bent near his partially conscious parent. "I shall pour you some tea, Mama. 'Twill strengthen you."

He lifted the steaming china teapot patterned in pink and blue flowers from a silver tray on the wooden circular stand beside the chair. Cups and saucers and a plate of fruit tarts in the same floral design, plus a small pot of honey, awaited use. The lady of the house must've been preparing to have tea and a snack when she'd detected their footfall on the stairs.

Not a servant was in sight. Someone had to have carried this repast to her, though. Colonial ladies of her social standing didn't cook or wait on themselves, unless they were impoverished. A glance at the well-furnished room bathed in dancing light told Lorna the Harrison family was anything but. Their fortune might change when the British closed in and resources were further stretched.

"Here." He poured a cup of the herbal scented brew, stirred in a spoonful of amber honey, and pressed it into his mother's tremulous hands.

Lorna recalled the lack of traditional tea during the revolution, and colonists making do with herbs. She also noted this was the second time he'd pressed a comforting cup onto a badly shaken female today. Well, today for her. Very English of him to do, despite being an early American.

Was there enough tea to go around, if she were introduced to the rest of the family and community? Might they need something stronger than herbal tea to steady their nerves when they met his zombie girlfriend, like kegs of whiskey?

She refrained from voicing this query aloud and sat where he indicated in the twin armchair beside Mrs. Harrison. The afflicted woman shrank toward her son who perched nearby on a long-legged stool, and away from his *undead* companion. Neither of them said a word to his freaked out mother, and he waited until she'd had a few sustaining swallows of whatever that stuff was before clearing his throat.

"I shall do my utmost to remedy the misunderstanding, Mama. Where's Adelaide?"

"Downstairs in the library," she said faintly.

He smiled. "My sister invariably has her nose in a book. Let's leave her there for now."

Lorna wished she could remember either of these females. Admittedly, there was a familiar quality about the elegant figure seated in the chair. The angle of her lace-capped head, the rustle of her skirts trailing the floor, the way she sipped from her china cup…stirred memories from the distant past. A lifetime ago.

Mrs. Harrison knocked back more of what sufficed for tea, then moaned. "When you shared your vision of a reunion with Lorna, I thought you meant in the hereafter. Not on earth."

A reasonable assumption, and one Lorna would have made.

The orange glow from the hearth played over Hart's intent expression. "I didn't understand what it

41

meant, only that we would find each other again. And now, we have."

Mrs. Harrison heaved a quavering sigh, followed by another weighty exhalation of air. If she'd had a well-endowed chest, she would have burst open her bodice, but she was small-breasted, like Lorna. "This cannot be, my son. Have you employed the dark arts to bring her back from the dead?" She shuddered and the whites of her eyes shown. "Is witchcraft at work?"

"Nae. Nothing like that, Mama."

"Just great," Lorna muttered. "I'll probably lose my job in my own time, and be burned at the stake in yours."

He angled his head at her. "Witches aren't burned in America. They're hanged or drowned. Not in years, as far as I know," he hastened to add. "Mostly, they're shunned. Although, with the war…" He didn't fully mask his hesitancy.

"Oh, that's very reassuring. Maybe they'll revive the witch trials. I want to go home now."

"You are home," he reminded her.

Still sheltering in his coat, she crossed her arms over the front of her sundress. "I'm from the suburbs of Norfolk. And I should have stayed there."

"You don't mean that, Lorna. You're just upset."

"You think? I get that way in tense situations, like discovering my life potentially threatened."

"Do not be alarmed. I shall explain you aren't a witch or that zombie creature you spoke of." He clasped his mother's narrow shoulder, his heartfelt expression imploring her. "Listen to me, please, Mama. Lorna isn't from the here and now, she's from the future."

She tapped a sandaled toe. "Like that explanation

ever works, Hart."

"It did with me," he pointed out, "when you suggested the possibility."

"True. But that's rare," she emphasized, it occurring to her that she'd never actually made this claim before him, only seen it flop in TV shows and movies.

Mrs. Harrison regarded her son blankly. "Have you taken leave of your senses?" She shook her head as if to shake off a dream, the eyes she swiveled at Lorna reminiscent of a horse demented with fear. "I'm having a nightmare and shall awake soon. Very soon."

Jeez. She hadn't ever been anyone's worst nightmare before and didn't relish the concept. "Better your mom thinks that, than the alternative. I see no way to convince her otherwise."

Everything in the hysterical woman's demeanor bespoke refusal to consider any other explanation. Granted, it was a lot to ask of the sorely tried lady. After all, Mrs. Harrison lived in an era with limited exposure to the concept of time travel. Lorna wasn't sure where the colonials stood on reincarnation, either. Hart was extremely adaptable.

He sighed, as if from his depths. This reunion among the three of them couldn't be at all what he'd envisioned. "I am grieved by your distress, madame." His tone was formal and detached compared to how he'd been with his mother before. She'd really let him down.

"Here's medicine. Take a few drops for your nerves." He reached inside his waistcoat pocket, withdrew a tiny glass vial, and uncorked it. "Slowly, mind," he cautioned, and tipped a trickle of the liquid into her willing mouth.

Cough syrup and cold medicine came in bottles, in Lorna's experience. "What is that stuff?"

"Laudanum. She's accustomed to this opiate. 'Twill help her sleep."

"I am asleep," Mrs. Harrison murmured, sagging back in her chair, the empty teacup in her lap.

Lorna thumbed at her. "One down. Anyone who ever knew me in this era left to go."

He slid the bottle back in his pocket. "She's a little high strung and prone to hysteria. I should have known better than to risk upsetting her. Others might react more favorably to meeting you."

"I wouldn't count on it. Fear of witchcraft is widespread in colonial America. Likely zombies, too, even if people aren't familiar with the term."

He shrugged, and loosed another sigh. "Not all are given to superstition. My sister, Adelaide, can be quite insightful."

"I'm sure she can. And I pity your mother, and hope she awakes with the belief that all this has been a bad dream. But right now, I'm not safe here." Lorna eyed the doorway, wishing for Doctor Who's *TARDIS* to make a hasty retreat. The DeLorean time machine would also work.

Get me back to the future before I'm toast!

****

Mrs. Hill's kind face swam into view. "I don't believe either of you have heard a word we've said."

We? Lorna joined Hart in surveying the former parlor, now a modern study.

Book cases stuffed with everything from antiquated leather-bound volumes to the latest thriller novels lined the walls. A massive desk sporting a state-of-the-art computer and touch screen glowed in the back, and she spotted a keyboard. She, Hart, Mrs. Hill, and apparently Mr. Cable sat in a semi-circle of expensive leather chairs before a homey crackle in the same hearth she'd previously stared into. He must relish a fire to have one going along with the air-conditioning. His electric bills had to be through the roof.

A serene blue-eyed Siamese, *Lyle*, she assumed, perched on the back of a mauve armchair contemplating her with feline aloofness. She jerked from her erratic thoughts and focused on the lean, lanky middle-aged man in the blue polo shirt and beige slacks seated beside her. *Between* her and Hart, actually, with Mrs. Hill on her right. Mr. Cable's thinning gray hair, glasses, mustache, and nondescript features, apart from his big ears, wouldn't have caught her attention, but his intelligent blue eyes flashed with enthusiasm. And he beamed at her and Hart. Here, was a man brimming with vision.

Wafting an agreeable spicy cologne, he clasped Hart on the shoulder and patted her arm. "Say you'll do it."

This time warp stuff was gonna be a real problem if it left gaps in their memory. She summoned a winning smile. "Could you please recap exactly what you have in mind, sir?"

Mrs. Hill shook her head. "Told you they were both dreaming."

"Of my proposal." He slapped his knee with a hearty laugh.

Lorna and Hart exchanged glances that said, 'Where in heaven or hell are we?'

45

Crossing both arms in front of his chest, the teasing man waggled a finger at each of them. "Not only are you two drop-dead gorgeous, you have acting ability. Hart, here, from his impressive reenacting experience, and Lorna from her roles in school theatricals." He grinned. "Bet you didn't think I knew about those, but I read your resume, such as it is for a high school graduate. I'm issuing an invitation to greatness. Join us in a tribute to the past history of Harrison Hall. You will be the stars." He flung his arms at the ceiling, as if to encompass the world. "Our production will be presented on Midsummer Eve. To be followed, of course, by the ball."

"Of course." Lorna had the sense she'd awoken in the middle of a play and didn't know her lines. Heck, she didn't even know which play it was.

Hart's stare mirrored her sentiment but he nodded. "I should be honored, sir. Shall I be portraying Hart Harrison?" His lips twitched slightly, at the irony, no doubt.

Mr. Cable bent toward him with an eager air. "Who else? Your resemblance to him is positively uncanny. And you've perfected the speech, dress, and mannerisms of his age. Your knowledge of the era is flawless, as are you. I admire how you stay in character, insisting on being called by his name."

"In truth, I am a Harrison, sir. I descend from the very man who built this house. 'Tis the family connection that has summoned me home."

"I well believe it. You have Harrison stamped all over you. Who else would have such commitment to the role you enact?" Like a tracking beam, Mr. Cable turned his admiration to Lorna, singling her out. "And this young lady is the epitome of her Randolph predecessor. A rare jewel."

"She is, indeed." Hart firmed the slight tremor at his chin, gazing at Lorna with the sheen of moisture he had before. "Unlike any other."

Losing her once must have affected him more deeply than she could possibly know. She imagined receiving word of his death, and fear clenched her heart in its icy grip. On impulse, she reached her hand across Mr. Cable to Hart and squeezed his fingers. He silently returned the gesture.

Mrs. Hill clucked. "It's plain we have a pair of lovebirds on our hands. And they only just met."

Lorna flushed and returned her hand to her lap.

"Love at first sight. All the better," their new champion crowed. "Think of the authenticity their relationship will lend the performance. People flocking to see them. This is the stroke of luck I've wished for. Prayed for, too."

But why? What was it all about? How had she and Hart found each other again, apart from the promise she didn't remember making, and his determination to find her?

How long would this togetherness last?

Forever, she hoped, while trepidation held her in its frigid grip.

Their fate was out of their hands. The house determined when and where they came and went without any apparent rhyme or reason. And yet, when she'd clamored to go back to the future, it had obliged her. Was Harrison Hall a living entity? Did it have an agenda?

She prayed the house was on their side. So far, so

good... *Please, let us remain together.*

Seriously? She was entreating a house?

"Hart, you will stay in the green room down the hall, and Lorna in the yellow room. Mine adjoins the study," Mr. Cable continued. "We recently relocated Aunt Jane to a refurbished cottage on the grounds, and Mrs. Hill has a modest apartment at the back of the house. This leaves an extra spot upstairs."

Hart seemed moved by the offer, and Lorna didn't know where he'd stay if the generous man hadn't made it. "Thank you, sir," he said, his demeanor respectful. "My chamber was originally downstairs. I believe my portrait still hangs there?"

"So it does. As for any thanks, the gratitude is all mine. I'm thrilled you've come to us." He clapped Hart on the back. "Consider yourself part of the family. In many ways, you and Lorna both belong here. She's descended from her namesake. As a Harrison, you are a vital link in the lineage of this house, though you won't divulge more specific details."

Hart opened his mouth in protest but Mr. Cable powered through. "I respect that. My gut tells me who to trust and what to do. How else do you think I've become a successful businessman?"

Lorna relied on inner guidance, too. Hart also must. Plus, he had a huge learning curve ahead of him.

"Mrs. Hill tells me you don't know how long you can remain with us, that the war may call you away. Well, I hope it lets you stay through Midsummer." For a lean man, Mr. Cable had a booming voice. "Can't have a play without the leading man, can we?"

And Lorna couldn't have a life if Hart left her.

"One other detail I should mention." Their

employer raised a cautioning hand. "You may notice some unusual activity in the house. We've had some strange occurrences." He forced a light laugh but the veiled concern in his expression betrayed him.

Mrs. Hill's twitter sounded contrived. "Hardly worth mentioning."

"Fair's fair," Mr. Cable said, waving her aside. "Only right they know. It's partly why I hired you so quickly, Lorna. That, and your name. And I'm delighted I did, now that we've met. Don't be overly alarmed if you catch sight of a person or persons who appear a little odd, or hear anything unusual. I assure you the spirits are quite benign. For some reason, we're experiencing the ebb and flow of paranormal phenomena from the past. Well, more than usual lately."

She and Hart exchanged glances.

"You've noticed something?" The watchful man shifted his nervous gaze between them.

She shrugged, and adjusted Hart's coat to keep it from slipping off. "An eighteenth century dance troupe in the foyer first thing this morning. Quite good, too. Especially one gentleman." She flicked him a wink, reveling in the heightened color in his cheeks.

"Really?" Mr. Cable stroked his mustache. "Wish we could get them to perform for our production."

"Maybe they will. Although, I could see partly through the figures. Like they weren't fully here."

"Ah." He nodded. "I get your point. Might be disconcerting to our guests."

You think? Having ghosts perform was unreliable at best, as were she and Hart. But she could hardly explain their strange circumstances without sounding bonkers.

"How about you?" Mr. Cable turned to him. "Noticed anything out of place since your arrival?"

His straight face that of a proficient actor, he shook his head. "Not a thing, sir. All is as it should be."

Impressive. The wink he gave her in turn nearly sent her into a coughing fit. She had that coming.

Their employer/host roared with laughter. "You two are gonna fit in here just fine." He thrust out his hand to Hart. "Agreed?"

He shook the man's hand, his gaze on her. "That is my fervent hope."

Clearly, Lorna no longer belonged in his world.

The gregarious Mr. Cable encircled an arm around them both. "I shall bless the day you came. What say you to some lunch, and Mrs. Hill will see about getting you both outfitted."

Hart appeared a little taken aback. "Won't I retain my uniform?"

"Certainly. However, you will also need civilian clothes. You weren't always a dragoon," the insightful man reminded him. "Especially, not when you first knew this fair lady." He nodded at Lorna. "Shall we head on downstairs?"

She was almost afraid to exit the room for fear of where she'd wind up but steeled herself. "As you wish." She was keeping a tight grip on Hart, though.

Mr. Cable squinted at her through his bifocals. "You look as if I'd invited you to your execution, rather than lunch."

The flames awaiting accused witches burned in her mind. *Not to worry*, she reminded herself, witches were hung or drowned in colonial America, or if she was really fortunate, scorned and shunned. *No biggie*.

"Not at all, sir. I simply wondered when you wished me to assume my duties." It was lame but the best excuse she could contrive on short notice.

He tugged the lobe of an overly large ear. "You mean what I originally hired you for? Scrap that, kiddo. I'll get another girl to fill in. One from the shop, for now. You and Hart have starring roles to prepare for, interviews to give, and crowds to charm. You up for it?"

"You bet I am." This would be the performance of a lifetime. And what better stage than Harrison Hall?

If the house would let them stay and play their part.

A thought struck her and she targeted Mr. Cable. "Wait. You mentioned more paranormal activity than *usual lately*?"

He lifted his palms in a shrugging gesture. "Harrison Hall always has some, dear girl. Ghost hunters get readings anytime they show up with their equipment. On those occasions I allow them in, that is. Pesky bunch."

"Has it always been this way here, do you think?"

The lines creased at the corners of his eyes and at his mouth. "I'm not sure. Possibly."

She searched Hart's penetrating gaze. He gave a slight but significant nod, meaning, *yes*. There was something about this house.

Chapter Five

Thank heavens. A modern kitchen. They were still in good old twenty seventeen and greeted by tantalizing fragrances.

Lorna could have dropped to her knees in gratitude. Instead, she swept through the door on Hart's arm. She must admit, his courtly manners were cool. He treated her like the lady of the manor. It might get old, she supposed. Right now—not a problem. Possibly not ever. She could get used to this. In fact, gazing through the frosted pane to her hazy past, she was accustomed to such genteel behavior in her former life. But sure as heck not in her current one.

Wow. She took in the sunny room, the red-checked curtains at the windows, red and white potted geraniums on the wide sills, and mellow oak cabinets throughout. The gleaming counters were blue tile, the appliances spotless stainless steel. Photographs of reenactors and events at the house depicting living history lined the white walls.

Smiling at Mr. Cable, she gestured at their cheery surroundings. "Very pretty, and patriotic with the red, white, and blue."

Hart lowered his puzzled gaze to her. "Why that?"

Their host snapped him a salute. "He's right. The Continental Congress didn't make the flag official until mid-June, seventeen seventy-seven. Hasn't happened yet in his day."

She couldn't imagine a time before Old Glory. "What about Betsy Ross?"

If anything, Hart seemed more confused. "Who?"

"Not famous yet," the resident historian added. "And possibly not even the original flag maker."

Lorna was dumbfounded.

"Never mind. A lot of fable is interwoven with history," he soothed. "Great catch, Lieutenant."

"Thank you, sir." His quizzical gaze circled the room. "This kitchen has magically appeared since my last stay at Harrison Hall. The chamber used to be a porch."

"Yes. It did. Funny you knowing that." Mr. Cable raised his hand, his lanky height nearly even with Hart's. "Never mind. Of course, you do. Aunt Jane built the kitchen on the back of the house, and I remodeled it. The eighteenth century version is preserved outdoors in the original building. We still cook in it almost daily to offer samples of colonial fare to our visitors."

He hailed the pleasantly plump, curvaceous, thirty-some-year-old woman in a white cap atop auburn curls and an apron worn over period dress. "What's today's sampling, Betty?"

"Gingerbread cookies fresh from the brick oven at the side of the big stone hearth." She expertly wielded a wooden rolling pin in pursuit of more pastry for pies. Half a dozen yummy creations cooled on racks, apple, blueberry, and pecan.

A smile curved Betty's freckled face. "By 'we' Mr. Cable means me and my staff."

"Guilty." He chuckled. "I don't cook. Not even to boil an egg. Lieutenant Hart Harrison and Lorna

Randolph meet Miss Betty Tallmage, our head chef. She's a miracle worker in the kitchen and invaluable to us. They say an army marches on its stomach. As do we. Betty, these two are our rising stars. They'll portray the originals of the house. Early Virginia gentry."

She gave a friendly, floury wave. "Pleased to meet you."

Lorna fluttered her fingers. "And you."

Hart dipped his head in a polite nod. "Good day, Miss Tallmage. Are you, by any chance, kin to the admirable dragoon officer, Major Tallmage?"

Lorna imagined Betty's surprise was typical of the response that would become commonplace with him. "From the American Revolution?"

"Indeed. Major Tallmage has distinguished himself."

She nodded, her hazel gaze searching the new arrival. "Actually, I can claim that distant honor."

He saluted her. "I've crossed paths with the major on some of our forays. Industrious women, such as yourself, keep the home fires burning while men like Tallmage are off fighting to forge a new nation. Your service is duly noted."

Her jaw dropped. "Well, thanks, Lieutenant."

Man, it wasn't enough that Hart was the best looking guy Lorna, and most any other girl, had ever seen. He was smooth, too. But she didn't question his sincerity for a moment.

"After weeks in camp, meals served indoors are most welcome, Miss Tallmage. Though I am accustomed to seating in the dining room when in my home."

Their host and employer smiled. "Certainly. You

shall dine there in splendor. Perhaps this evening." He bent his six foot plus frame nearer to Mrs. Hill, who stood considerably shorter than he did. "I'll get Bill in to take shots of our couple at various functions. Maybe a day long shoot."

Hart drew Lorna closer with a protective arm. "Why do you wish this Bill to fire on us? Even in pretense, such farce is dangerous."

"Not musket balls, Lieutenant. He will take photographs of you." Wonder tinged the humor in Mr. Cable's eyes. "My, you do stay in character. I read Daniel Day Lewis didn't break character for three months when he played *Lincoln*."

"Amazing," Lorna inserted, before Hart asked who Lincoln was.

"And annoying, I'll bet," Mrs. Hill added.

Feigning deafness, Lorna gestured at the pictures on the walls. "These images are like portraits, Hart, only much faster to create."

The tension at his jaw relaxed. "Ah. There is much for me to learn in this new world."

"Indeed." Their host punched his shoulder playfully. "And no, the camera doesn't capture your soul." He grinned at the old superstition.

Hart didn't loosen his hold on Lorna. "I most assuredly hope not. Mama is ever concerned over potential devilry."

No freakin' kidding.

"She'd be appalled by most television programs—" Mr. Cable broke off. "Never mind. TV's not in your memory bank."

"Speaking of memory, I believe you forgot these, Lieutenant Harrison." Mrs. Hill pointed at the leather sword shoulder carriage worn by mounted dragoons, and the sharp rapier itself, suspended from the arm of a wooden chair in the kitchen corner. A powder horn hung alongside them. The heavy leather hat, shaped like a helmet, with brass trimmings and a long horsehair crest held the place of honor on the seat. A cartridge box and metal canteen rested beside it. The haversack and knapsack for rations and personal items were stowed on the floor by the chair legs with the bedroll. A short-barreled carbine was propped nearby.

She tilted her capped head at him. "Not Miss Tallmage's usual paraphernalia."

"No," Betty tittered. "Think you left these things on the bench in the foyer. The staff brought them here for safekeeping."

Hart flushed. "Pray forgive any inconvenience I may have caused, Miss Tallmage. Having no immediate need of my arms and equipment, I unburdened myself upon my arrival in the house."

Dang. Lorna was impressed. "That's a lot of stuff to carry."

He shrugged. "Worse for the infantry. I tie neat bundles of the baggage behind the saddle and shoulder the rest." He turned toward Mr. Cable, pivoting Lorna with him. "I rubbed Rock down, watered him, replenished the hay, and left him in the stable with the other two horses. He occupies a loose box. I trust that's suitable?"

"Perfectly. You could hardly leave him in the entryway along with your gear." Their lanky leader gestured at the large rectangular table covered in a red-checked cloth. "Please. Take a seat. Visitors aren't allowed back here, and crowds are thin today. I've got one of the girls from the shop conducting tours, freeing Mrs. Hill to better devote her attention to you. We'll discuss more of what I have in mind as we dine."

He peered at the couple clinging together as if for dear life. They kind of were, given that Lorna feared being swirled away from Hart at any moment, and he was bent on keeping her safe.

"Perhaps you two would be comfortable there?" He indicated two chairs at one side of the table. "The rest of the staff have eaten. It's just us four. Pork barbecue, coleslaw, potato salad, and homemade buns sound good to anyone? There's pie for dessert."

Hart smiled. "I thought there might be."

"Ladies first." Mr. Cable gallantly sprang ahead and pulled out a seat for Lorna.

She'd never been treated so royally. "Thank you." She slid into place, fresh gratitude welling in her.

Not only was she glad for the meal, and thrilled to have Hart at her side, but relieved to dine without accusations of witchcraft hurled at her. Always a plus. Given the choice between his wailing mom and the British Legion during the revolution, she'd rather take her chances with the latter.

Mr. Cable seated Mrs. Hill, who adjusted her skirts as she settled in the tall-backed wooden chair at one end of the table. He sat at the other end, like host and hostess. Lorna understood the housekeeper to be a widow. She didn't detect any particular affection between the two beyond an amiable work relationship, though. Their shared goal of furthering recognition for Harrison Hall was also a common bond.

Betty wiped her hands on a white kitchen towel and bore platters of food to the table. The aroma of fresh bread sent Lorna's stomach into rumbles, and the spicy meaty fragrance of the barbecue was to die for. It had been a long, long morning. She'd ventured back in time without more than a cup of tea to sustain her.

The renowned cook gestured at the food. "We serve family style here. Help yourselves while I get drinks. Will ice water do you?"

Hart lifted shocked eyes. "Water?" She might as well have offered him a glass filled from a polluted stream. "No ale?"

"We slipped up," Mr. Cable conceded, with a smile. "Colonists drank like fish. When soldiers ran out of rum, they declared there was nothing to drink. Get the man a beer. He probably prefers it warm."

"Is there any other way?" Hart asked.

"Yeah. Cold from the fridge." Betty handed him an uncapped beverage.

He recoiled slightly at the chill in his grasp but raised the bottle to his lips.

"We've got sweet iced tea, too," she added.

Hart winced at the offer.

Lorna lifted her hand. "For me, please."

Cubes clinked in glasses and Betty handed round the frosty beverages, with pitchers ready for refills. "I'll brew a fresh pot of coffee. Mr. Cable drinks his by the barrel. You have heard of coffee, Lieutenant Harrison?"

"Yes, Miss Tallmage. And I have sampled the beverage. I prefer hot chocolate."

"Whatever you like." Obliging Betty turned away, probably to search the cabinets. Hot chocolate was more of a winter drink.

Maybe coffee hadn't yet been perfected in his time. Lorna couldn't recall. No matter, she was ravenous. She took the dishes, ladling mounds onto her white china plate, then passed them on. Clinking spoons, forks, and knives sounded against rapt dining.

"So good." She offered between mouthfuls, blotting her lips on the snowy napkin. "Betty, you're a culinary genius."

"I get that a lot." She laughed, trotting the coffee pot around for seconds. "How do you find the fare, Lieutenant?"

"Admirable. I shall recommend you to General Washington."

"Hold on, we don't want her stolen away." Mr. Cable swooped on the aromatic brew in his cup. "No one makes coffee like she does, either. We'll coax you round to a cup yet."

When the avid diners paused for a sated second, he gestured for attention—probably to deliver a speech, as fired up as he was about the newcomers.

Smiling on them like Santa Claus, he swept his spectacled gaze over Hart and Lorna. "Ah, my golden…" He circled his fingers while searching for the word, as if to snatch it from the air. "I want to say my golden *children,* without causing offense. I'm hopeful we shall become like family, and I'm old enough to be your father. Think of me as parent, boss, and director all rolled into one. A kind of *Father John.*" His eyes brimmed with zeal behind the square frames.

Before they ventured a response to this unexpected sentiment, he spurted ahead. "Do either of you sing or play an instrument?"

A little erratic the way he shifted subjects but geniuses were often eccentric. "I sing." This much, Lorna reluctantly divulged, not the years of piano lessons. She'd suffered through annual recitals since age six. Playing before the crowds *Father John* envisioned, didn't bear contemplating.

Hart raised a tanned hand. "I sing, if you require a baritone accompanist for Miss Randolph."

If possible, the visionary's smile broadened. "Splendid. And I play all manner of piano and stringed instruments, and am a prolific composer. You both act and sing, anything else to add to your accomplishments?"

"Fight, when needed." Hart was matter-of-fact. "You are acquainted with my horsemanship?"

"By reputation. You're said to be superior, according to accounts." Mr. Cable scrutinized him. "Do you, by any chance, fence?"

"Yes. All true gentleman must be acquainted in defending themselves with a sword. Mine is in the house." He frowned. "Somewhere."

"What about that one?" Lorna pointed at the rapier hanging from the back of the chair.

Father John waved aside her find. "Not a fencing sword, dear girl. Those are longer and far grander. Often family heirlooms."

"Mine is, or was," Hart muttered.

The older man rubbed his chin. "Left it in the house, you say? I'll have the staff search. Visitors are restricted to the downstairs and a few outbuildings. Theft is rare. I can't imagine someone staggering to their vehicle with such an immense find and no one noticing. It should turn up. But do have more care in future. Valuable to you, is it, Lieutenant?"

"Highly. A gift from my grandfather, Sir Thomas Harrison. He built Harrison Hall."

"Of course." Mr. Cable and Mrs. Hill exchanged inquiring glances.

Either Hart's superb rendition of the original Lieutenant Harrison continued to impress them, or they were beginning to wonder if he fit somewhere into the unexplained paranormal activity.

Lorna guessed he'd left his sword in the seventeen seventy-seven version of the house, and had no clue if the heirloom remained on the premises. The pucker at his lips said as much.

Back to fencing. *Wow.* In addition to everything else, he did cool stuff with swords? Could he be any more awesome?

Next question: How could she hold onto him?

Everything hinged on the house, and whatever will it was working.

A jolting thought occurred. "How did Hart Harrison die?"

He jerked a startled gaze at her.

Mr. Cable cleared his throat. "I assumed you both knew."

She tensed every muscle and hardly dared to breathe.

Hart better hid his emotions. "How can I know what I have not yet experienced, sir?"

"Touché." Mr. Cable removed his glasses, wiping them with a napkin, every moment an agony to Lorna. "Sadly, Lieutenant Harrison died young. You'd think he'd have fallen in battle if this were the case. But, no, he was felled in a duel."

She gripped the edge of the table. "When?"

"During a visit at Harrison Hall on Midsummer Eve. At the ball. In seventeen seventy-seven."

A shockwave ricocheted through her.

He glanced enquiringly at Hart. "The very year you chose for reenacting."

Jaw clenched, he met the older man's quizzical regard with a level stare. "Curious, that. Swords or pistols?" he asked, his voice a little gruff.

"Hmmm…" Mr. Cable rubbed the tip of his nose. "Swords, I believe. Although, pistols were popular in that era."

Mrs. Hill nodded. "Yes, I recall something about swords. Lieutenant Harrison chose, you see, when the challenge came."

"Who killed him?" Lorna forced the query from her tight throat.

"The disgruntled nephew of a neighbor, a Mr. Theodore Archer," the housekeeper supplied. "His family called him Theo. He had few friends."

She hated him already. "Why did he strike Hart down?"

Mr. Cable restored his glasses, and considered them with a pensive expression. "Jealousy over Lieutenant Harrison's accomplishments is the general assumption. Hart was well thought of in the community and regiment. No doubt, he'd have made captain before long, had he lived."

Lorna couldn't believe they were discussing the vibrant young man seated beside her.

Father John drummed his fingers on the table. "I'll need an actor to portray Theo Archer. Someone who can fence."

The furrow between Hart's brows deepened. "How did a swordsman as accomplished as Lieutenant Harrison lose to an inept neighbor? Worse, die from his injuries?"

Mr. Cable scratched his balding head. "There's some confusion surrounding the event. The annals don't say. However, his second in the duel accused Theo of cheating. He was even more unpopular after the fatal encounter and moved to New York State following the war."

"So I should hope." Lorna wanted to go back in time and finish Theo before he had the opportunity to challenge Hart.

"I'm surprised he wasn't tarred and feathered," the resident historian added. "That being the practice of the day."

Mrs. Hill crossed both arms over her ample chest. "I'd boil up the tar."

Lorna pictured her stirring the kettle, but this didn't alter the outcome of that fateful encounter. An idea flashed in her mind, brilliant in its simplicity. The duel had not yet occurred in Hart's former life. It loomed a little way ahead. If he remained in the present, perhaps he could avoid an untimely end?

Determination swelled in her. She must persuade him to stay here, if the house would allow. Surely, it hadn't brought them together only to tear them apart again?

How cruel a fate would that be? Only, this time round, she'd be the one grieving his loss, rather Hart shattered over her death. Angst pitted in her suddenly leaden stomach.

"Ready for pie?" Betty chimed in.

God, no. Lorna bit back. How could the woman think of pie now? "No, thank you, Betty. Your fabulous meal filled me to the brim. Perhaps later?"

The dessert invitation was lost on Hart. He stared straight ahead, likely weighing his options, and none too pleased by any.

Mrs. Hill contemplated the quiet young man. "He really takes his role seriously, doesn't he?"

"You have no idea." And Lorna wasn't about to elaborate.

Sympathy mixed with the curiosity in Mr. Cable's close study. "I've never met anyone like you, Hart. It's an honor to make the acquaintance of one so dedicated to preserving the past. History must be appreciated by people of all ages. You can help make that possible. Are you with me?"

He lifted eyes gone gray. No blue showed. "To the death."

"*No.*" Of that, Lorna was determined.

Mr. Cable's puzzled gaze met her resolve. "But he does. Theodore Archer fells him. He may have cheated to do it. Probably did. But there it is. How else can our program go?"

She clenched her hands in her lap. "Find a way."

"What? Alter history?"

"Answer me this, would Hart have died if he'd had modern-day medical intervention?"

"Possibly not. But we can't rush an ambulance to the scene and spirit him away to the hospital." He attempted a laugh. It fell flat, as if he'd chuckled at a funeral.

If the boss man couldn't intervene, maybe she could. First, she had to pull herself together, or they'd have her committed. "I'm sorry for being this emotional. I just get so caught up in their lives."

He nodded, and Mrs. Hill murmured sympathetic

noises.

"I understand wanting to alter events. Especially when you're deeply invested in a role." He studied her, his expression thoughtful. "But you didn't know you were to play Lorna Randolph until today."

"I didn't realize a lot of things, but I'm learning fast. This place gets a hold of you and sinks in."

"I hear you." Father John stroked his mustache. "It's like Harrison Hall awoke and has something to say."

Yeah, well, the house was gonna have to change its story. No way, it was bringing back this amazing guy and then snatching him from her again. She understood the expression, 'Scream the house down,' because that's what she wanted to do.

She wasn't losing Hart. The end. Whether the force driving the strange activity in the house was for them, or against them, she didn't yet know for certain. But she was doggedly single-minded. They would prevail.

Chapter Six

Whew. Wee. Wow. If they harnessed Mr. Cable's energy, he'd generate enough current to power the estate. Three cups of coffee hyped his buzz. Now, he was downing his fourth refill of the aromatic black brew. A high octane idea's man on caffeine electrified the kitchen.

He'd moved past the fit Lorna pitched over Hart before reining herself in, and proceeded with his plans. Which was good, as he wasn't focused on her. But he was like a hyper kid, galloping his fingers over the table and up and down his arms while he spoke. He paused to interlock them before him as if in prayer, then flung his hands, palms open, at the couple.

"Here you both sit, the epitome of your ancestors, and I didn't even know you existed until today." He waved at them. "Not with these looks, I didn't. No one gave me a heads-up about Lorna, let alone Hart. I wish I'd realized sooner I had such prodigious talent available to me. We have much to do and scant time to do it. Costumes, Mrs. Hill." A chopping gesture to his palm accompanied this directive.

Her tranquil expression resembled the serenity of a saint. "I'll see to the clothes. You make your arrangements."

"We need added man and woman power." He pounded his fist on the table, rattling the dishes. Betty jumped at the sink. Lorna had braced herself. Hart must have nerves of steel from the war, and the unruffled housekeeper didn't even blink. "Only a few short weeks remain until Midsummer. I want to show off my two stars well before then, and long after. We may be talking movie here."

"Seriously?" Lorna hadn't just gone backward and forward in time, she'd landed on another planet.

"Sure. I have contacts and prospective investors. The sky's the limit, as far as I'm concerned. How better to snag people's interest in the house than with a tragic romance?"

She wished he wouldn't refer to them that way.

Oblivious of anything beyond his scheme, he squared his fingers in the shape of a camera lens and panned the couple. "Speaking of love, the camera's gonna love you two."

"Doubtless." Hart eyed him as he might a madman he was attempting to placate.

"You don't know what a movie is, do you, Lieutenant?" Nothing got past Mr. Cable.

"Not in my *memory bank*, as you termed it, sir," he reminded the would-be producer.

"It's moving pictures." Lorna danced her fingers in front of him. "Like a play, only if we're in the movie, we can watch ourselves. Awesome."

He slanted dubious eyes at her. "Magic?"

"No. There's a scientific explanation, which escapes me."

A thoughtful pause stilled their excitable benefactor, likely the lull before a storm. "Bill will elaborate when he comes. He's a wizard with film."

"As I suspected. Magic," Hart muttered.

"Pardon the expression, Lieutenant. I didn't mean a real wizard," Mr. Cable amended. "We're not talking Merlin. Bill's a genius."

"Ah." Hart shrugged compliance with this explanation.

It intrigued Lorna how Mr. Cable played along with his *reenactor staying in mode* veneer, unless he had an inkling the eighteenth century dragoon really was from that time period. Hard to tell.

"As to the clothes," Mrs. Hill soldiered on, battling to return them to the subject. "We have several period gowns for Miss Randolph to try, until more can be made or found. We have a gentleman's suit for Lieutenant Harrison, though he's rather tall. I'll get their measurements after lunch."

"We'll need several changes of wardrobe each." The impatient grate was back in their commander's tone. "And another officer's uniform. I'd like to see him in the really striking blue faced with red coat and waistcoat adopted by the Virginia dragoons." He turned to Hart. "Do you have a problem with that?"

"Not if you want a uniform that screams 'shoot me.' I blend better with the countryside in my brown and green."

"But you aren't blending with it. You're starring in a performance." The corners of Mr. Cable's mouth turned down in a pout.

Mrs. Hill intervened. "He's a bit of a *fashionista*, our Mr. Cable. But I agree. Red and blue would show up better in the production and in photographs. Some dragoons adopted those colors earlier than others, didn't they, Lieutenant Harrison? Even Colonel Bland wore it for full dress."

"I wouldn't venture into battle decked out like that, and dare say Bland wouldn't either. But if you wish me to don the uniform for show, then certainly." He patted his side. "I shall need my sword. An officer always wears one."

The smile returned to Father John's blue gaze. "Never fear. We'll turn the house upside down in our search."

Lorna feared the house would do that on its own. She still wore Hart's coat around her shoulders and hugged it close in the air-conditioned chill.

"Hire whatever costume designers and help you need pronto," Mr. Cable rapped at his unflappable assistant. "I want the clothes and uniform ready yesterday."

Hart startled. "Are you venturing back in time to accomplish this end?"

"Only an expression," Lorna interjected.

"A peculiar one. You have a great many of these oddities."

"I'm sure you have some baffling expressions in your era, too," she argued. "What about *Yankee Doodle Dandy*?"

"The song?" He smiled. "That originated with the British soldiers. Now, we also sing and dance to it."

"But the lyrics make no sense. What does 'stuck a feather in his cap and called it macaroni' mean"?

"A macaroni is a dandified fop in a huge wig, tight jacket, and breeches, his face powdered and cheeks rouged. That verse is a jibe at rustic colonials, as if they think sticking a feather in their skin caps makes them fashionable."

Mr. Cable applauded him. "Excellent explanation.

I'm off, my golden ones." With a final gulp of coffee, he pushed back his chair and launched into action. "I have no end of calls to make. I must get in touch with Bill…" Muttering to himself, he strode out the door. "Meet back here for coffee and a briefing at four thirty. Show me what you've got."

Mrs. Hill grunted a confirmation. "That's him in full sail. Bill O'Neill is his right arm and the man behind the camera. He's short and rather squat, the opposite of John Cable. Some call them *the odd couple*. We three best be on our way. Costumes are stored on the third story, in what was formerly the attic. Mr. Cable remodeled it."

Of course he did. "I have the impression he's restored or redecorated most everything," Lorna observed.

"Pretty much. Poured a fortune into this place. But he loves it, and I don't know what Lady Jane would do without him. You'll meet her later, she lunches early and rests in the afternoon."

Before Mrs. Hill stood, Hart was on his feet, easing back her chair. "Why, thank you, sir." She rose with his gentlemanly support and waved to Betty. "See you later. Betty and her second-in-command, Alice, outside now, are two of the lucky ones who share a bungalow on the grounds," she added for the newcomer's benefit.

Betty grimaced. "Yeah. That way we can get in more cooking." But she didn't really seem to mind.

Hart swung around and assisted Lorna to her feet. She was perfectly capable of rising unaided; it was the possibility of venturing through the door to another era alone that had her bracing against him. Not that she didn't savor his touch beyond the protection he offered.

Tiny shivers darted through her at his nearness. Her heart doubled its speed, both from trepidation and being next to him.

He took her arm with his natural flair and gestured her ahead in a ducal flourish. Together, they followed the woman skirting up the hall. Fragrance accompanied their passage. The sweetness of roses emanated from the pink petals in the china bowl on a side table…honeyed beeswax candles mingling with their floral perfume. But these pleasing scents, and the charming rooms she glimpsed, didn't ease her apprehension.

She tugged on Hart's sleeve to slow their pace. "I'm not looking forward to heading back up those stairs, and possibly into your world."

"It was once yours, too." A wistful note hung in his hushed reply.

"Hazy centuries ago," she reminded him.

"Not for me. Little more than two years have passed since your death. Yet I understand your reluctance."

"*Reluctance*? Try terror. Your mother thinks I'm *undead*. Others may also. I'm even afraid to go to the bathroom alone, for fear of where I may wind up." She stopped to think. "You don't have bathrooms in your time, do you? How about a privy?"

"Ah. Yes. The *necessary*."

"It's indoors now, instead of an outbuilding. I'll show you." Another thought occurred, and her cheeks heated. "How bizarre if we have to go to the bathroom together to keep from being torn apart."

He smiled. "A chamber pot is stored under your bed if you prefer, or a close stool stands nearby to sit upon."

"An old-fashioned potty chair, huh? Neither are available in this era."

"How inconvenient."

Lorna raised her eyes to the incomprehension in his. She was communicating with someone from a different time period and culture. "We're gonna have to get you house trained."

"Like a dog?" He snorted.

"Seriously, Hart. What are we to do about our predicament? Besides, my adamant resolve to keep you away from that duel."

His mouth creased in grim lines. "I will not participate in my own demise, if it can be avoided. As for the ever-present danger you face in the past, if I must be by your side while you attend to private functions, I shall turn my head."

"And cover your ears, and possibly your nose."

His lips twitched.

"Oh, crap. We cannot behave like Siamese twins."

"Which are?" he prompted.

"Literally inseparable. And crap no longer means what it used to in your day."

He arched his brow in feigned shock. "Are you slipping vulgar terms into our conversation, with me unaware?"

"Only a few."

Mrs. Hill cleared her throat. "What is keeping the pair of you?" She waited ahead of them, foot tapping, at the base of the steps.

They approached her arm-in-arm, nervous tension crackling between them like static electricity. The way the house switched time periods was rather like the changing staircases in *Harry Potter*. Lorna didn't know from one step to the next where she'd be. Neither did Hart.

The housekeeper must've mistaken their clinginess for an inability to detach for a second and shook her head at them. "Young love is truly amazing. Didn't you two only just meet?" Mirth hinted at her mouth, and an 'I'm too old for this' expression crinkled her eyes.

"No. We didn't. We've known each other since childhood." Odd, Lorna making this confession, when she couldn't recall more than teasing glimpses of her former life. However, her swell of emotions for Hart went beyond conscious memory to an instinctive bond. If souls had mates, he was hers.

Mrs. Hill considered them. "Harrison Hall is host to a reunion, is it?"

"Of sorts. We haven't seen each other in years." This much was truthful. At least, regarding Lorna. She didn't need to cross her fingers behind her back, and saying they hadn't seen each other 'in centuries' might be a bit dramatic.

"You're making up for lost time mighty fast," the astute woman observed.

"We kind of have to."

She hitched her hands on padded hips. "Why is that?"

How could Lorna explain?

He laid a cautioning hand on her shoulder. "Our new roles under the tutelage of Mr. Cable have thrown us much together. But you may trust me to conduct myself as an officer and a gentleman, madame."

Humor touched Mrs. Hill's pale blue gaze. "Don't let that spoil all your fun. You're only young once."

Actually, Lorna had discovered she was young twice now. She couldn't trot out that piece of information, though. Neither did she want to ascend the steps with the housekeeper, and risk a repeat of this morning's strange occurrence while in her company. Better they went on their own. Plus, she really needed the bathroom after all that tea.

She gestured the woman ahead. "Please, go on. We'll meet you in the attic. I want to refresh myself first."

"Very well. Take a short break. I'll sort through the clothes and see what we've got. There are some costumes from our last event left in the wardrobe in your bedroom, you might want to check." She gave a congenial wave. Lifting her skirts, she started up the steps. "Also, you might be interested to learn the cupboard tucked under the stairs is what used to be called a *water closet* with modern amenities. A term even Lieutenant Harrison may recognize."

A smile tugged at his lips. "Indeed." He waved Mrs. Hill out of sight, then swept his hand at the hidden bathroom. "After you, my lady."

She eyeballed the diminutive restroom. "We can't both fit in there without squashing together. Promise you'll wait for me just outside the door with your hand on the knob. That should keep us connected, if I grip the inside knob." She thrust his coat at him. "You might as well put this back on."

He shrugged into his uniform. "Go. I shall man my post."

Lorna ducked inside. Tending to her personal needs was a challenge with one hand on the knob. She managed as fast as was humanly possible. The flush shook the compact space. She wriggled into her panties, and took turns washing each hand, chaffing at every second they were apart. She didn't dare release the knob. What if he disappeared, or she did?

Voices murmured beyond the door. Visitors to the house, maybe. "Hart?" she tested, to be certain he was still there.

"Present and accounted for."

Was there a slight strain to his low reply?

"Come out when you're finished and meet my sister, Adelaide."

Chapter Seven

"Holy crap." The expression escaped Lorna before she could stifle her response.

A masculine chuckle sounded from the other side of the bathroom door. "What is holy about crap?"

"Not a lot."

"Heavens above. She truly is inside," a woman, who must be Adelaide, uttered in shocked tones.

"Did I not say?" Hart, and presumably his sister, conversed in stilled voices, while Lorna endeavored to smooth her skirts with one hand.

She fished in the small purse slung over her shoulder, drew out a brush, and ran it through her shoulder length hair. Awkward lip gloss application followed, and a spritz of vanilla perfume.

"But 'tis fantastical, brother," Adelaide replied, to whatever confidence he'd made about their quandary.

"Indeed." His acknowledgement carried through the wooden partition.

"I agree with whatever Hart said." Maintaining her hold on the knob, Lorna opened the door, and emerged into the darkened hall lit only by flickering candles.

Night had fallen in the past, which was fitting, really. The scents were similar, beeswax, roses, and a new one, jasmine. Adelaide's perfume, she assumed. "Is it June, seventeen seventy-seven, here, too?"

He nodded solemnly.

So their times had synched, though not the hour.

Not releasing her link to the future—this cubbyhole might be the portal—Lorna met the fascinated blue-gray gaze of his younger sister. The same chestnut-brown hair as his was pinned in curls on her head, and a tier of pearl drops hung from her shapely ears. A blue gown with an embroidered stomacher at her middle, and lace flounced sleeves, fitted her perfect figure and swept the floor. She wore a gray and blue printed shawl around her slender shoulders. While her sibling was tall, she wasn't above five feet two inches.

The two girls stared at each other, faint memory stirring in Lorna. *Yes*, she had known this petite beauty. She and Adelaide were the same age, eighteen going on nineteen. At least, they had been once. Hazy impressions of Adelaide floated through her mind, barely more than the distant memory of a scent. And yet, it was something.

"Lorna? How is it you stepped from the cupboard beneath the stairs?" Adelaide muted her voice, presumably not to waken her mother or the rest of the household.

"Look." She opened the door a little wider to allow her entranced spectator a peek inside. The fixtures were still visible. "It's a water closet. I just flushed the toilet and ran the faucet."

Adelaide seemed as hypnotized by the amenities, possibly more so, than by Lorna's return from the dead. "That must be the gushing liquid sound I heard."

"The noise brought her trotting from the library." Hart gestured at the room down the hall on the same side as the parlor. He didn't release his hold on the outer knob, which had him standing next to Lorna, one on either side of the door. "It's a library still."

"Good." To her growing appreciation, much of the house remained unaltered, restored by the dynamic Mr. Cable.

The wondering girl bent nearer the bathroom. "How does this water closet work?"

"You sit there." Lorna directed Adelaide's enthralled attention to the white commode. "There's toilet paper for after." She pointed to the white roll. "You push that metal handle when you're finished, and it flushes everything away."

The wowed spectator sucked in her breath. "Miraculous."

"Not quite. It's called plumbing." She navigated in the space suited to a tiny house and turned on the tap.

Water gushed forth, and Adelaide exclaimed. "May I try?"

Lorna shot Hart a questioning glance. "Will it carry her to the future?"

"Who knows?" He smiled indulgently at his sibling. "Go ahead. Enjoy yourself. It's little enough to ask, stuck at home as often as you are during the war."

"True." She should help, not hinder, her long-lost friend's curiosity.

She and Hart stood like sentries at the door while the petite young woman swished into the bathroom. Laughing like a child with the most out of this world Christmas present ever, she ran her fingers under the tap and splashed her poreless complexion. "Can I do the flush?"

"Sure." She'd never seen anyone, above the age of two, this excited about water whooshing away in a downward spiral.

Adelaide clapped her hands. "'Twould astound King George himself." Blinking wet lashes, she swiveled her starry gaze at Lorna. "Is this what the future holds?"

"Yes. Though not in your lifetime, I regret."

The mesmerized girl gestured at her sundress and strappy sandals. "No corset, or sleeves? Half your legs and toes exposed. Are you attired in the fashion of the new age?"

"I'm no fashion queen, but yes, eventually this will be typical of summer style. There are many other changes in the world. Lifesaving medicines will be discovered. And electricity. Lamps turning on at the flick of a switch." She opted not to explain space shuttles and computers. That would be tough enough for Hart to comprehend.

"Is it not all marvelous?" Adelaide might have been in *Wonderland*.

"Yes. I suppose it is. We take these, and many other things, for granted in the future," she admitted.

The wonderstruck fan of all things modern dried her fingers and blotted her face on the hand towel. "How did you get there?"

"I was reborn in the year nineteen hundred and ninety-eight. The question is, how have I returned here, and how is Hart journeying forward to the future?"

Wisdom shone alongside the awe in Adelaide's gaze. "And why?"

He shook his head. "All we know is the house shifts us between Lorna's new life and her old one with us."

His sister didn't question his assertion, or Lorna's reality. A wistfulness crossed her eyes. "Why does it not take me forward? I should like that."

"Perhaps it will. If you encounter a Mr. Cable or Mrs. Hill in the future, tell them you're a *reenactor*," he advised, "one who portrays the past, and they will be delighted and endlessly entertain you."

An expression of reproof firmed his sibling's countenance. "Is this what you have told them?"

"It's what I have allowed them to think. Traveling between time periods is unsettling for most folk. Better to accommodate their expectations with a reasonable explanation, than to rattle them unduly."

Lorna lightly squeezed Adelaide's arm. "If your mother mentions seeing us together earlier today, please insist the visitation was only a dream. The sight of me deeply disturbed her. We left her sleeping in her chair."

"That was you? She has made such an assertion. With the laudanum, I assumed it to be a vision borne of opiate."

Hart nodded gravely. "That was my intention, and that others do the same. I gave her a calming dose before we left."

"This was not today with Mama, but yesterday," she argued.

He sighed. "Time is unpredictable, its course changeable, in this back and forth shift. 'Tis yesterday afternoon in the future. At least, it was, a short while ago. I pray we return before many moments pass."

Adelaide weighed him. "What of your life with us, and your duties to the regiment, and the cause? Papa battles on."

"I do not doubt that for an instant, sweet sister. I am ever loyal and would see my service through." He hesitated.

"But?" she prompted.

"I can scarcely believe it myself, having only recently learned, that my time here is soon to be cut short."

Her mouth dropped open. "How can you possibly know this? Have you consulted a seer?"

"No. My death is recorded in the historical accounts left of me. Mr. Cable has read these documents."

She gaped at him in disbelief.

"Adelaide," Lorna summoned, before the house spun them away again. "Listen to me. Hart is to die in a duel with Theo Archer on Midsummer's Eve. We must prevent this. If we are returned here on that fateful evening, will you help us in any way you can?"

"With all my heart. Tell me how?"

"I cannot say for certain. Remember, medicine and doctors are far advanced in the future. Come what may, Hart cannot remain here, but must return there. This, I know. Take your cues from us, and let instinct be your guide."

The floor creaked overhead and footsteps echoed.

"Hush," he warned. "We must have wakened Mama. Make haste, Lorna. Back inside the water closet."

Adelaide fluttered her fingers. "I shall contrive an account to satisfy her curiosity, and may the Lord pardon my deception."

"I'm sure he will." Lorna caught his arm. "Squeeze in here with me, or we may be separated. Goodbye dear Adelaide, if this is our parting. I do not recall our last one."

She nodded dazedly. "You faded with fever. There

were no final words for me. You whispered Hart's name."

The image her bygone friend painted gave her a pang, and they exchanged glances ripe with emotion. "It's but the shadow of a memory. While your face, Adelaide, returns in my thoughts."

She smiled through glistening eyes. "Thank you. I hope we meet again. Though, not on Midsummer's Eve. What of you, brother?"

"We can but stand in readiness." He clasped his sister's hand then released it and crammed into the minute space behind Lorna. Neither of them made an effort to hold onto the knob, only to each other. The press of his strong body sent ripples shimmering through her, distracting her from fear of detection.

"Pray excuse the intrusion on your person," he whispered, tightening his muscles to lessen his crush on her.

"Not your fault." She spoke in the most hushed tone possible, and him still hear her.

She arched backward to allow him slightly more room, and he closed an arm around her waist to prevent her from falling onto or into the toilet. His eyes twinkled with mirth. Despite everything, the humor in the situation wasn't lost on him, or on her, for that matter.

"If we are about to be discovered, 'tis a most incriminating posture," he said softly. "Perhaps we should make use of it?"

Their lips were mere inches apart, and it seemed the most natural thing in the world when he closed his mouth over hers.

Scorched seconds followed, with every part of her

incinerated by the inferno he ignited. The fire raging between them both exhilarated and frightened her in its intensity. Amazing how much emotion could be exchanged between two people without heaving a sigh. They muffled their pants, and the rise and fall of their racing chests pressed together. She'd never been this intimate with anyone in the whole of her two lifetimes. Not her loser ex-boyfriend. No one. The passionate exchange between her and Hart in this cramped space, constrained by the need for quiet, was also the most romantic she'd ever experienced.

Surely, someone must overhear them, no matter how they tried to muffle their desire? She stifled a gasp when he slid his lips to her neck, and elicited exquisite tremors.

He relented before she gasped more loudly, and pressed light kisses over her cheek, returning to her ear. "I want you more than I can say." A velvety hiss only she could hear.

Thank God, she hadn't slept with that rat of a boyfriend, because she badly wanted to give herself to the love of her life, well, her last life. The consummation never took place because they were cruelly torn apart. Hart was fast proving to be the love of this life as well.

She eased an arm around his strong neck. "I want you, too. There are no words for how much."

"You need none."

He covered her mouth again with his, and she thought she'd explode into a thousand pieces like the stars across the heavens. Good thing this tiny compartment was air-conditioned, or they'd be overcome by heat.

The thread of voices outside the door intruded on the hottest make out session ever, and he drew back, a finger to his lips. Whoever these people were, they conducted an indistinct conversation. Gradually the buzz grew distant, and faded into silence.

She exhaled slowly. "Think it's safe to leave?"

He grunted an affirmative and pressed his seductive mouth to her ear. "We cannot possibly remain in here. After promising Mrs. Hill I would behave with honor, I have taken every advantage of you. Forgive me."

"There's nothing to forgive." How she wished they could lose themselves in each other with no thought for propriety, or anything else that dictated behavior.

Being nearest to the door, he turned the knob and cracked it. The hall shone with mid-afternoon light streaming through the windows. He opened it farther. "All clear."

Relief washed through her. "We're back in good old twenty seventeen."

"Shouldn't that be *new*, not old?" He ducked his head and stepped from the compact room meant for one.

She followed him, tidying her hair and attempting not to appear like a girl who'd done exactly what she had. "It's a spin on the quote from a movie about time travel."

"You must show me one of these movies you and Mr. Cable refer to. Perhaps then I may also make clever allusions."

A thrill charged through her. "What fun that would be. Maybe later they will allow us some R and R. Rest and relaxation, or is it recreation?"

He arched his brow. "I am not certain what *recreation* they have in mind, but I shall endeavor to contain myself and behave properly."

She wished he wouldn't and wondered how she'd handle a full blown, head-over-heels, love affair. A volatile part of her burned to discover, while the other wanted a ring on her finger first. Whether this hesitation arose from teachings in this life or the former one, she wasn't sure. But caution tugged at her.

Who the heck? A couple approached in attire suited to the century she and Hart had just exited. Or had they?

The gentleman wore a russet coat, gold waistcoat, brown breeches, white stockings, and gilt shoes with shiny buckles. A gray wig covered his head beneath a brown tricorn hat, and he carried a walking stick. The woman on his arm rustled by in gold taffeta, emeralds at her ears and throat, and a white powered wig beneath a wide hat encircled with ribbons.

Hart bowed to the fashionable pair. "Good afternoon, Mr. Dare. Mrs. Dare."

"Afternoon," the man rumbled, returning the polite gesture.

The lady dropped a short curtsy. Lorna attempted the same in her sundress. No more was said, and the couple strolled on by them, never batting an eye at her outlandish attire. How was that possible? She was totally unsuitable for the era they depicted, unless they thought her a visitor. Were they reenactors, or not?

The instant they were out of earshot, she nudged Hart. "Are we back in time again?"

"Not unless that era is haunted, too." Taking her arm, he strode toward the stairs, putting distance between them.

Chills shivered through her. "What do you mean?"

"Mr. and Mrs. Dare are deceased."

Her stomach clenched. "More of that paranormal activity Mr. Cable mentioned?"

"Exactly." He escorted her, trembling, up the steps.

"But you handled it so calmly."

He shrugged. "So did our specters. Fortunately."

Mrs. Hill frowned at them from the landing, layers of cloth draped over her arms. "What on earth is keeping you? Don't tell me it takes this long to visit the bathroom?"

"I feel as though this day has gone on for years," he muttered to Lorna.

For him, it kind of had. Felt more like a wild week to her.

"Ghosts, my good woman," he said aloud. "And visions from the past."

"Well, if that's all." She beckoned to them. "Meet me in Lorna's room. I have some clothes for you both to try, and I need to get your measurements. Come along. Don't be shy." She trotted off.

He shot Lorna an arched look. "Just as well we shall have a chaperone for this disrobing exercise."

"We won't always have one, and I'm afraid to let you out of my sight."

At first, his widened gaze reflected bemusement, then laughter hinted. "If we are sharing the same bed, I cannot vow eternal chastity."

Nor could the quivering girl at his side. "I suppose it's a little early to announce our engagement?"

He regarded her as if he could not believe his ears.

She clapped a hand to her mouth. "Oh, I'm sorry. I

assumed you still wish to wed me, but if you don't—"

Pausing on the steps, he circled an arm around her waist and drew her close. She nestled against him with a sigh.

"I have found you, my lady," he whispered. "I knew I would somehow, somewhere, though such thoughts were deemed madness borne of grief by others. Let us satisfy Mr. Cable's expectations and find a way to prevent my imminent demise, before we make an announcement."

She spoke past the lump rising in her throat. "Sensible strategy. Must be how you made lieutenant."

"It's said I could have made captain. Maybe even colonel."

"Yes," she agreed. "No telling how far you might rise in the ranks. But discussing your military career is futile at this point. My college plans are a distant swirl. Our main goal now is staying alive."

"You already died and are reborn."

"I could die again. Particularly in *not* so good old seventeen seventy-seven."

"Hush. I won't allow it." He silenced her with a quick kiss, sending quivers through her. "Onward in our battle campaign. We march to Mrs. Hill in the yellow bedroom."

"Kind of like the murder game *Clue*: Mrs. Hill in the bedroom with a coat hanger. I'll explain later about that, and a whole lot of stuff." If the house allowed them the time they needed for Hart to soak up info and make plans together.

Any sort of *together* would be bliss. But she longed for the really alone kind.

Chapter Eight

Hart lowered his long frame onto one of two gold armchairs before the dark hearth in Lorna's room. He turned the seat to face her. "What do you think of your bed chamber?"

Antique furniture restored to pristine condition by Mr. Cable, filled the generous space. Taking pride of place in the center was the four-poster canopy bed overhung with gathered lengths of white ruffled cloth. Not only were the furnishings outstanding, but she appreciated the unique touches that personalized the room. This one had presence.

She gave an encompassing wave at the opulence around her. "Fit for royalty."

"Not quite that extravagant, yet among the finest in Virginia," he said with a note of pride.

Colorful gowns heaped the ivory coverlet bordered in blue forget-me-nots. These dresses were from Mrs. Hill's first foray to the attic. The harried woman was off making a second run, with instructions for the couple to *stay put*. She'd had enough of them, 'disappearing, God knows where.' So had Lorna, and hoped the house would allow them a respite.

"It's beautiful." A short candleholder with a single taper, meant for carrying if need be, stood on the circular nightstand by the bed. She also noted an oil lamp modified for modern life with wiring for electricity, and discreet outlets. Sensible adaptation.

Along one buttery wall, a tall dresser laden with drawers waited to be filled. A stately wardrobe rose beside it. The weighty piece of furniture nearly reached the ceiling. Afternoon sunlight streamed over the white dressing table with an oval mirror and cushioned stool in front of the window.

On the top of the vanity was a silver-handled brush, comb, and handheld mirror. Exquisite perfume bottles of different shapes and colors, and diminutive china pots added more feminine touches to the surface. Face powder, rouge, and sweet-smelling salve were stored in the ornate containers. The pleasant violet scent from one opened pot perfumed the air.

A gilt-framed portrait of roses, daisies, and forget-me-nots also brought the outdoors in, as did smaller floral paintings. She turned slowly, taking it all in. "It's as if I've stepped back in time to the genteel bedroom of a special lady."

"You have. Yours."

"Really?" An indescribable sensation of knowing, and yet, not knowing stirred in her. She strove to think back, back, back. "Were the walls always yellow?"

"Yes. To lighten your spirits."

"They do." The sun-dappled hue was cheery. "What of the forget-me-nots? They not only border the ivory coverlet, but the curtains at the window. Were they always here?"

"Not the same fabric from over two centuries ago. This is a reproduction. Mama embroidered the flowers on the cloth to remember you by..." He trailed off, huskiness roughening his voice. "I came in here once to see her handiwork. That was all I could bear. Until now."

"Oh." Chills scattered tiny prickles over her. What could she say to the raw pain in his eyes?

She must've died in that bed. Probably not something she should bring up. She didn't recall her passing, anyway.

Pregnant silence hung between them. Then she gestured at the paintings. "Were these here?"

He singled out the large portrait with forget-me-nots in the mix. "Mama commissioned that one to be done…after."

Lorna swallowed hard. "She truly must have loved me to do all of this."

"She did. Still does. And now, she's about to lose her only son."

"Oh, no." Lorna was resolute. "We'll find a way."

His eyes were gray pools of emotion. "Whether or not I escape my fate, I shall be dead to her."

She opened her mouth to argue, then shut it again. He couldn't remain in that era after his predetermined demise, or it would alter everything, the entire fabric of the future. And she would be left in this world without him. Unthinkable.

"True. You will be gone. Technically, you already are. But I get what you mean." She walked shakily to where he sat and sank into the other armchair, angling it toward him. "I have little memory of before. Bits and pieces, like the color yellow…maybe that dressing table. It's so strange my being here now."

"And my being with you. We are cut from irregular cloth." He entwined his warm fingers with her chilled hand. "Remember, 'There are more things in heaven and earth, Horatio. Than are dreamt of in your philosophy.'"

"*Hamlet*. Act one, Scene five." She spoke automatically. "I played Ophelia in Community Theater."

"Ah. The Bard continues in popularity?"

"Shakespeare is immortal."

"'Tis good to know."

She waved her hand in a sweeping gesture to encompass the house. "It would seem Harrison Hall never forgot you."

He eyed her pensively. "Must be why I'm here."

Mrs. Hill bustled through the door, cloth spilling over her arms to her knees, and intruded on their profound exchange. She huffed to the bed, waving at Hart to stay where he was, as he'd gotten to his feet in deference to her arrival. Technically, she wasn't 'a lady,' but he showed respect for her place in the household.

"I've left gentleman's clothes in your room, Lieutenant Harrison. If you would be so good as to try them on. And leave your uniform on the chair for me to have it cleaned. We send costumes to a specialty drycleaners." Speaking over her shoulder, she heaved the load beside the rest and smoothed the fabric with a loving pat. "Mr. Cable wants us back in the kitchen for our next rendezvous. Betty is serving supper in the dining room. Bill and his camera are joining us this evening, and you will meet Lady Jane. I mean Mrs. Randolph." She pivoted, inspecting him with a critical glint. "I suggest a shower and a shave."

He eyed her blankly, probably wondering what constituted a shower in this era, and envisioning a walk in the rain.

"I'll show you, Lieutenant." She spoke with the weary patience of one tolerating a consummate actor. "Your things have been relocated to your room. Have you anything else we may have overlooked, besides the sword?"

"No. My knapsack, haversack, and bedroll hold everything I carry with me on the campaign. Dragoons travel light."

"Yes. Yes." She pressed her fingers to her temple, apparently to ease a headache.

Go figure.

"You will find basic toiletries in the bathroom cabinet," she continued. "Use those until more can be provided. They are suitable and likely preferable to whatever you're packing. I've hung a white terrycloth robe on the back of your door. I don't suppose you have any night attire?"

He shrugged the obvious. "My shirt."

She sighed. "Colonial men sleep in those long-hemmed creations, but I suggest you not wander the hall in that scant attire. Please don the robe for such ventures, or if you have the urge for a midnight snack."

A frowned furrowed the corners of his eyes. "I shall observe decorum, madame. And we do wear banyans, similar to a robe. Mine is not among my gear. 'Tis in this house. Somewhere."

"Quite right. Forgive me. Would I be correct in assuming underwear are not in your vocabulary or your possession?"

"Under...wear," he mused, as if trying to connect the term to an item of clothing. "My shirt," he tried again.

"I see this is as near as we're going to get. Purist

reenactors don't stoop to boxer shorts, but I'm adding them to the list of miscellaneous apparel to be purchased for you."

"You're making a list?"

Lorna failed to suppress a smile at his bafflement.

"I am," the take-charge female wore on. "I trust you two don't mind sharing the one bathroom on the hall? Mr. Cable has his own, as do I in my compartment."

Hart's muddied expression brightened. "The water closet? No. Not at all. I shall stand guard for Miss Randolph."

Mrs. Hill raised her eyes heavenward. "Excellent. We may be attacked at any hour, and certainly don't want the young lady caught unawares in her bath."

"The British are not yet this far south, unless you have received word?"

"No. Best to be prepared." The stoic humored him.

His manner serious, he nodded. "It is, in any event."

With this, Mrs. Hill made no argument. "Right then. Let's get you situated. You can shower while Miss Randolph tries on her costumes." She cocked an eye at Lorna. "You're daisy fresh and should do as you are for the evening's festivities."

She stirred in her chair. "I showered this morning. I'm happy to assist him, Mrs. Hill." Hart couldn't possibly know about plumbing.

Her eyebrows arched. "In the shower?"

"No, no. With the knobs and such. Then I'll go."

The exasperated woman stabbed a finger at the bed. "I want you in those clothes. I'll be back in a minute to help you do the laces, ties, and check on the fit."

"Be sure he understands how the cold and hot faucets work. They can be tricky for one so long in camp," Lorna added, in an attempt to justify his ignorance, fearing he'd scald himself. He'd better tolerate the ice cold blast.

Mrs. Hill fixed her with a martyred expression. "If that Daniel Day-Lewis fellow can refuse to leave his prop wheelchair, and have the crew carry him around and spoon-feed him while they filmed the movie where he's supposed to be handicapped, like I read he did, then I can manage an explanation of the shower for Lieutenant Harrison."

Lorna was out of arguments. She squeezed Hart's hand, and shot him an imploring look. "Be careful, and return to me."

"Heavens above." Their chaperone threw her hands up. "He's only bathing and changing clothes. Not going into battle."

That's what you think. He might end up back in time without Lorna, as might she in his absence. And there was a war going on in that era. All hell could break loose. Nothing for it other than to steel herself and pray the house cooperated.

At least she didn't pray *to* the house, just *about the house*. With this faint consolation to her Anglican conscience, she watched him follow Mrs. Hill out the door. He cast her a backward glance and mouthed, 'Wait for me.'

She mouthed, 'Always.' Their steadfast pact.

Chapter Nine

While Lorna wondered how Hart fared and *where*, Mrs. Hill tightened the corset laces at her back. "You are a wealthy young lady from the seventeen seventies, and must dress appropriately if you're to play the part with conviction."

Being roped into stays, an earlier word for corset, was an ancient rite she faintly remembered. Her modest chest swelled as the form-shaping garment pushed her breasts into mounds. No wonder memory stirred. This is what the original Lorna had endured, probably without the inner voice crying, 'No way. Why can't I just wear my strapless bra?' She thought she'd gone all out with underwire beneath her sundress.

The costume mistress nodded her satisfaction. "Now you'll better fit the gown. Designed for a particular shape."

The one Lorna was being molded into, she supposed. She'd already donned the elbow and knee length linen shift beneath the corset, and had been allowed to keep her panties, while reminded they did not yet exist in the eighteenth century.

She glanced down at her corset and shift. "What did they wear beneath their gowns besides this?"

"Not underwear like you're thinking. Nice and airy below." Mrs. Hill smiled, then grew brisk. "Let's get this in place." She tugged at the ruffle edging the neckline of the shift, also called a *chemise*—so many interchangeable terms—until the decorative trim peeked above the stays. "Good. Now for the petticoats."

Lorna stepped into the plain white garment, and her assistant tied it in back at her waist. Next came the blue outer petticoat, more of a decorative skirt, with a wide ruffle at the hem. "Two petticoats?"

"Oh, my. Ladies often wore more than that," her assistant/torturer emphasized, smoothing folds, "and hoops or panniers along with them. They had to turn sideways to get through the doors."

"How did they sit?"

"They didn't. We're not adding that much fullness to your gown. And now, for the *pièces de résistance*," which Lorna recognized as French for 'the showpiece.'

Wreathed in smiles, Mrs. Hill held out the burnished cascade of whispering fabric for her to rustle into. "I wish I could wear this," she sighed, fingering the folds like lost treasure.

So did Lorna. Despite its ribboned, lacey, shimmering glory, the dress wasn't what she'd consider complete. A wide swathe cut below her bust showed everything from there on down. She glanced at the worshipful woman. "Seriously?"

"The gap at your midriff closes with a stomacher." Mrs. Hill triumphantly inserted an intricately embroidered V-shaped panel, secured with hooks and eyes hidden beneath the gold trim at the sides of her gown/bodice. "The blue skirt is meant to show." She clasped her hands together. "Isn't it splendid?"

Lorna angled this way and that, studying her reflection in the dressing table mirror. The orange-gold gown shone like sunlight, the blue skirt was the sky, and the embroidered flowers on the stomacher formed a garden. Her fitted sleeves ended in wide flounces, the same shade as the gown. She had the posture of royalty because the corset forced her to stand up straight, and the bust she'd never thought she had, showed rather well. Comfy? No, but…

Tilting her head at Mrs. H., as she'd begun to think of her, she nodded. "The overall effect really is quite spectacular."

The eager woman beamed, then cast an anxious glance at her feet. "What of your shoes? Do they pinch?"

"No." They were ridiculous, patterned with flowers and adorned with big bows, while embroidered garters held her white stockings in place above the knee. But they fit.

"Good." Her costume obsessed companion stood back, rubbing her chin, and scrutinizing her handiwork. "We need a bauble at your décolleté."

"My what?"

"Revealing neckline, dear." She fished in the carved wooden box hidden beneath the flounces, silk shawls, and multi-colored ribbons on her bed.

Out came a three strand pearl necklace with a blue sapphire encased in more pearls dangling at its center. A tier of the small white globes, like teardrops, hung from the stone and completed the magnificent setting. Mrs. H. fastened the lengths around Lorna's throat. The pearl drop sapphire—surely, a fake?—nestled above her rounded breasts. Matching sapphire earrings completed the dazzling ensemble.

"Perfect. Have a care with the jewelry, my girl.

The gemstones are real, and these pearls aren't plastic."

She sagged under the weight of such responsibility. "I shall guard them with my life."

"Let's hope it doesn't come to that." Mrs. H. preened over the effect for a moment, then rushed on. "Hair up in a bun and I'll get the wig."

"Wait. What?"

"Your own hair won't do." She trotted to the wardrobe and took out a large white box. From the crinkling folds of tissue paper, she lifted a white-blonde wig, styled in curls pinned on top, with several artful loops descending. "It's well made and beautifully arranged."

And massively more hair than Lorna actually possessed. She stood speechless while her fairy godmother twisted her shoulder length hair into a bun, and settled the queenly creation on her head. More patting and primping followed. And *oohs* and *ahhhs*.

"Well?" Bright-eyed with her achievement, Mrs. H. nodded at the mirror.

Lorna stared at her reflection. "I look like a debutante attending her first ball. One of those helpless historical sorts. Or Marie Antoinette. Dang. She lost her head."

Mrs. H. snorted. "You're exquisite. As to helpless, well that depends on how well you can manage in this getup, and keep your wits about you. Tell you what. I might have something to lend you more girl power."

Her curiosity was piqued. "What is it?" She'd portrayed some ditzes in plays before. Ophelia hadn't exactly been with it, poor thing. Empowerment was cool.

Again, Mrs. H. dipped back into the carved box.

"Here you go," she said, and pulled out a short-barreled pistol. "It's a prop," she added, at Lorna's gasp, "but looks like an eighteenth century ladies' pistol."

"Sure does." Especially as she hadn't seen one before. "Where can I put it?"

"In a reticule, or purse."

"They had those back then?"

"Oh, yes. Mostly for a scent bottle, handkerchief, fan, gloves, that sort of thing." Mrs. H. pivoted back to the pile on the bed. "I have one here. We can get more selections in, if you prefer. Ladies also carried large bags for their knitting and sewing. You are more the purse sort."

Considering she'd never knitted or plied a needle in her life, she agreed.

Mrs. H. held out the heavily embroidered bag made from sturdy purplish cloth with a drawstring closure, suspended by a loop of lavender ribbons. Some woman had been busy plying her needle. "You can wear this over your wrist, possibly even your shoulder. Unless you want a different style?"

"No. This is awesome. Thanks." Lorna stuck the pistol inside the bag. "Kind of heavy, but it works."

Mrs. H. smiled. "Whatever makes you happy."

This was news to someone strapped into a corset. But she couldn't expect to wear her sundress and call it period dress.

"Mr. Cable wants you done to perfection for round one of the pictures this evening. Some powder and a dab of rouge on your cheeks, I think." Her costume, now makeup, mistress scurried to the nightstand.

Lorna's jaw dropped. "Isn't that stuff ancient?"

"We have replaced the contents since the

eighteenth century. This collection isn't just for show over here." Shaking her head, Mrs. H. returned with a brush in each hand. On went a dusting of face powder, and more than a touch of color on her cheeks, she suspected.

"Must do your lips." Her assistant darted back to the vanity, stowed the brushes, and dipped her finger into a pot. "Your predecessor would've used a preparation of dried red beetles, finely ground, to color her cheeks and mouth."

"I'll bet Lorna number one didn't know that."

"Probably not. Rest assured, we have advanced cosmetics." Mrs. H. slid the color over Lorna's lips and wiped her hands on a handkerchief. "Ladies didn't wear eye makeup back then. They sometimes instilled belladonna drops in their eyes to make the pupils larger."

"Isn't that poisonous?"

"It can be," she said matter-of-factly, and handed her the mirror from the vanity. "Take a good look."

Lorna raised the glass to reveal an eerily familiar face peering back at her from over two hundred years ago. If the original Lorna had dressed for a ball or dinner party, this is how she would have appeared. The hair might have been her own, if she grew it to her waist. The rest was identical.

"You must smell the part." Mrs. H. spritzed her with a blend of jasmine and she didn't know what else.

Fragrance charged the air. Her presence would be detected before she entered a room.

The zealot tapped a finger on the perfume bottle. "I can't think of another thing."

"A stirring film score for the movie I'm in." She

felt as if she were about to star in one—and lose her head.

"Doubtless, Mr. Cable will play for us this evening. Wouldn't be surprised if you and Lieutenant Harrison will be expected to dance."

Panic stirred. She couldn't emulate the dancers she'd seen earlier today. "I don't know how."

Mrs. H. patted her shoulder. "Instruction shall begin."

"What if I need to go to the bathroom?"

"You've been. You have a young bladder. Hold it." She took the hand mirror and laid it aside, then pointed at the stool beside the dressing table. "Sit there, while I round up Lieutenant Harrison. Since we're running late, Mr. Cable said to forego our meeting in the kitchen and go straight to the dining room." She patted her cap. "I ought to change. Meanwhile, don't mess anything up."

Like a five-year-old admonished not to muss her party dress, Lorna lowered her rustling layers onto the stool.

"I'll knock on the lieutenant's door in passing and tell him to come escort you to supper. Honestly, when you aren't accustomed to walking in those long skirts, you'll appreciate an arm to lean on. He'll keep you from falling down the stairs. The occasions I've nearly taken a tumble…" Chatting away, Mrs. H. hastened out the door and shut it behind her.

Well, Lorna might not be able to manage the steps, according to her mentor, but she was *packing*. This day, now evening, was like a bizarre Halloween, only it was June, and she was dressed as herself—her former self. Nothing odd about that. Heck no. She'd just sit here waiting on her time traveling boyfriend. Lord only knew what he'd been up to.

A rap on the door disrupted her self-talk.

Hart. Chest fluttering with anticipation, she lifted her skirts, all three layers, and darted across the room.

She turned the knob and—her spirits plunged. An unfamiliar gentleman stood at the threshold. She might not recognize him, but his attire didn't originate in this century, or the one before that, or that… He was fully corporeal. She couldn't see through any part of him, so he probably wasn't a ghost.

Crap. Had she gone backward in time, or had he come forward?

He surveyed her from beneath swarthy brows, his black eyes traveling over her in seeming surprise and interest. Male admiration was gratifying after all her efforts. However, his 'take her now' demeanor was a little unsettling. Maybe he was a pirate? And what was with the white wig? He wore the false hair tied back at the neck with rolled curls at either side of his face. Absurd, and a shocking contrast to his olive skin.

"Forgive the intrusion, madame. I was advised this chamber was empty. There's an overflow at the Turner Home where I am staying. They suggested I seek lodging here."

She attempted a calm reply. "As you can plainly see, the room is occupied, sir."

"I humbly beg your pardon, fair lady." He bowed in a formal bend of the waist, lowering his substantial figure. He must be nearly as tall as Hart, his forest green suit of superior cloth and faultlessly tailored.

Mrs. H. would be impressed.

Lorna dipped a curtsy in acknowledgement of his apology. Formalities observed, she raised her head.

He flashed her a smile, revealing white teeth in a not unhandsome face. Hart's teeth were also white but this man's contrasted more forcefully with his complexion. He appeared of Italian or Spanish descent, or was one of the 'dark' Irish, those brooding Celts. A charisma hung about him. But his English carried no distinguishing accent.

"Pray allow me to introduce myself." He offered a shorter bow, which she reciprocated. "I am Mr. Theodore Archer."

Dear God. The man who killed, or was about to kill, Hart in the duel. She nearly stumbled back.

Instead, she held her ground, clenching her bag, and slid her gaze to the sword at his side. Did all gentlemen walk around with a sidearm in that era? She couldn't recall. Even so, it didn't bode well. If she felled him here and now, she might prevent the duel.

Black brows arching, he awaited a response.

"The name is known to me," she forced between her teeth.

He probed her uncertainly. "Not disagreeable, I trust, on such short acquaintance? I wish no offense to such a divine lady."

Flatterer. She'd like to throw him to the floor in a swift martial arts move. If she knew any. Perhaps a less hostile approach would better suit her purposes.

"Heaven forbid." She forced a light laugh. "Pray allow me to make introduction. I am Miss Lorna Randolph."

He extended a gloved hand. "My honor to make your acquaintance. Pray forgive the circumstances of our meeting."

"Of course." She touched her fingers to his.

The tilt of his head, and his musing expression, suggested he knew who she was. "Forgive me. Did you say *Lorna* Randolph?"

"Why, yes. It's a family name."

His gaze tightened. "That is impossible."

"How so? Do I not stand before you?"

"The lady by this name is…"

"What?" she dared, grit edging her tone.

"No matter." He brushed off her query and the accusation on the tip of his tongue. "There must be a misunderstanding."

"Concerning what?" She twirled around, her gown a swirl of bronze with orange highlights. "My death?"

He paled. "You jest."

"No. I was buried. I am returned." She pulled the pistol from her purse. "You may not be so fortunate."

His staring eyes said more than words ever could.

"There's someone I would like you to meet. Turn around and we shall cross the hall to Lieutenant Harrison's chamber."

He pivoted. "You are mad—"

She shoved the barrel in his back. "And you are a dead man, if you don't cooperate. Now, march."

Before they exited her room, a stunned Hart appeared in the hall outside the door. He glanced at either side of the passage, then gestured for Lorna and her prisoner to retreat. Stepping after them, he secured the door so no one could see.

She had a brief moment to appreciate how his blue coat brought out the color in his disbelieving gaze. Sleek gray breeches fit his muscular legs above black dress boots. He must have insisted on this detail, rather than shoes. And she approved of his glossy brown hair pulled back at his neck and tied with a black ribbon.

He swept his gaze over her with a mix of 'Lorna?' 'Wow.' and 'Have you lost your freaking mind?' in their depths.

He waved both hands at her. "What in God's name are you doing?"

"Taking Mr. Theo Archer prisoner, until we can best determine where to dispose of his body."

Hart stabbed a finger at the stunned man. "That is not Mr. Archer."

"What?" A jumble of images and words swirled in her mind. "But he said he was, in plain English, after appearing uninvited at my door."

"If I might be permitted to speak," the supposed Archer interjected.

Hart shifted his frown between them. "Lower your pistol, Lorna. It's not real, sir, as any *gentleman* could see. Pray continue, Mr.?"

"Brady. Sam Brady."

"And do not neglect the reason for your presence in Miss Randolph's bedchamber, Mr. Brady."

"Gladly. John Cable and Bill O'Neill thought it would be a hoot for me to begin my acting gig with a bang. They didn't mean *literally*. I'm an acquaintance of Bill's, who recruited me to play the part of Theo Archer in the upcoming production. Anyway, the whole thing was their idea. Who knew she'd take me seriously?"

He spun toward her. "Why did you think I was the real dude? The guy's been dead for over two hundred years."

She stuck the fake gun back in her bag. "You're not the only actor on site, dumb ass."

"No need to be abusive."

"Oh, there's every need. And don't pull that crap on me again. Didn't Mr. Cable tell you about the ghosts here?"

"What the hell?" His expression was pure satisfaction to witness.

"Ask him—"

Hart's stern eye halted her in mid-sentence. He'd led men into battle, fought against the most powerful military force in his day, and was fast rising in rank. Judging by the narrow look he shot her, she got why. Her faltering gaze lowered to his side, and the sword she hadn't noted with all the distraction.

She snapped to attention. He'd made another trip back in time.

He motioned to their supporting actor. "After you, Mr. Brady. We shall join you anon. I would like a word with my lady."

And what a word it would be. Her legs shook. Sitting down might be a wise option.

"I eagerly await her next act." The fake Theo left on the tail of that snarky comment.

Hart considered her in gaping wonder before saying a single thing. "You were prepared to kill him?"

"In my own defense, I should point out I was strongly considering imprisonment."

"If that failed?" he pressed.

"Well, technically, he's already dead."

"Not this particular gentleman."

"The real Theo—"

He raised a hand, cutting her off. "We need to establish rules of engagement."

The term was vaguely familiar. Oh yeah. The

movie. He probably meant something else.

Fixing her sternly, he continued. "Do not kill or maim civilians. Unless they pose a significant threat."

"I thought he did."

"*And*," Hart wore on. "Are in their own time period. *And* have committed an act that constitutes an attack."

"What? You want to wait to be attacked now? You know it's coming, from where, and by whom."

He eyed her as if she spoke a foreign language. "Firstly. If you alter events of the past, for example, slaying a man before his appointed hour, you might tear a rip in the fabric of the universe. Secondly, when did you grow to be such a firebrand?"

She tensed at his reproof. "Why? Did you prefer the first model? I live in an altered world and have had totally different experiences from the young lady you knew."

The severity in his gaze softened slightly. "Tell me. What has changed you, Lorna? You have the same beauty and charm, and yet, you are not the same girl."

"No. Unlike Lorna number one, I am not the cherished ward of a doting family, but one of four daughters in a busy household with never enough energy or funds to go around. I relied too heavily on my cheating ex-boyfriend—disloyal suitor," she amended for Hart's benefit, "who professed undying love, then betrayed me with my best friend. Which means she also stabbed me in the back. Figuratively speaking."

Halting to gulp a breath, she searched his eyes, creased in sympathy, and gained the courage to continue. "The affair between them, and the cut to me, resulted in a lot of drama, or gossip, making life at home impossible and drove me here. To this house. With you."

"Where you belong," he said softly.

Her lip quivered. "And I don't ever want to be without you. So, yes, I considered doing away with the man who said he was Theo Archer. Only, I wouldn't have the faintest notion how to go about it. I cringe at squashing bugs. And would probably tie him up with ribbons,"—she waved at the bed—"and leave him in the wardrobe. No rope, you see…" she trailed off. "I was bringing him to you."

What would he say? She waited, blinking at the unwanted moisture in her eyes.

Unbelievably, his lips twitched. Then an unmistakable smile curved the edges of his sensuous mouth. More incredible, he threw back his head and laughed.

"Not from the injury to your heart and honor," he sputtered, between inhalations. "Never that. But the vision of the man tied with ribbons in a ladies' wardrobe." He slapped his thigh and bent double. She'd rarely seen anyone this overcome by mirth.

He finally regained some control, mopping his eyes with a handkerchief from his coat pocket, and gasped. "Forgive me."

She smiled wryly. "I suppose I had that coming."

"Whether or not you deserved my hilarity, you received it graciously." He held out his arms. "Come here."

Snatching up her skirts, she ran to him, leaning her head against his solid chest and hugged him close. The position was awkward in the wig, and she had to keep her red cheek from smudging his coat. "We mustn't mess ourselves up, or there will be hell to pay."

He wrapped strong arms around her. "I know. They await us below stairs. We have but a moment, and must join them."

"Hart," she whispered.

"Yes?"

"Don't die. Promise we'll find a way to stay together."

"I will do all in my power, my lady."

"What if it's beyond your power? What if there's something I must do?"

"Then God help us."

She socked his arm. "You might be surprised what I can accomplish."

"I already stand amazed."

Mrs. H. skirting through the door put an end to any further exchange. "You two are coming to the dining room this minute if I have to haul you there by your ears."

"Not necessary, madame." Hart turned Lorna around, her skirt swaying, and took her arm. "We are ready to proceed."

The irate woman paused, the annoyance in her eyes giving way to admiration. "Damn. Don't you make a fine pair?"

He inclined his head graciously, and Lorna held to him, praying they arrived at their destination in Eastern Standard Time, two thousand seventeen. They swept from the room and down the hall behind the female billowing ahead in fuller skirts and a fancier lace cap than this morning. She'd dolled herself up for the evening, seventeen hundred's style.

"When did you retrieve your sword?" Lorna

whispered.

Hart bent his head nearer hers. "I found myself in my former time again, and the household asleep. I slipped into my bed chamber downstairs and searched. The blade lay on top of the dresser. Left in that spot, I assume, by my mother, or one of the servants."

Alarm twinged in Lorna. "You could have been stuck back there. How did you return to me?"

"I discovered the water closet, or cupboard, truly does work as a conduit between our two worlds. At least, for us."

"That's good to know." This portal might prove to be a lifesaver.

"Ah. Look who we have here," he said under his breath.

They made their bows to Mr. and Mrs. Dare as they passed the ghostly pair on the stairs, unobserved by Mrs. H. sailing ahead.

A chill froze Lorna. "Why do the Dares keep appearing?"

"Perhaps they are come to attend the ball?"

She cast a shivery glance over her shoulder at the couple vanishing into mist. "Midsummer is several weeks away."

"They are dead to us both. And do not observe the timely progression of events."

"Will more attendees show up?" A disturbing thought.

"Perhaps. The ball is the highlight of the year. Until Yuletide. Christmas," he added, at her apparent confusion.

"What happens then?"

"Another ball."

"Will we always have ghosts, do you think?"

He shrugged. "I have no notion what will happen in the next instant, let alone *always*."

"Neither do I." Part of her was excited to discover what lay ahead, and the other, equally terrified.

Chapter Ten

Her skirts brushing the polished floor, Lorna swept into the dining room on Hart's arm. Relief welled in her upon discovering the expected assembly seated at the magnificent table. A dazzling array of blue and white china, crystal goblets, and gleaming silver lined the snowy cloth. White tapers burned in tiered candleholders, and white lilies and roses filled the lavish centerpiece. The scent of flowers mingled with fresh bread and ripe apricots.

"My time," she whispered.

Hart paused with her inside the doorway. "Fast becoming mine, too."

"Yeah." He must feel as if he were on a crazy merry-go-round of worlds. She surely did.

Sam Brady's mocking smile didn't delight her. At least, he belonged in this era. Getting to his feet, he offered them a less than sincere bow, which Hart curtly returned.

"The smug-faced brat," she hissed.

Hart laid a cautioning hand on her arm.

Mrs. H. beamed at her charges as if she'd created them, and waved from the far side of the table. "Here they are."

"Miss Randolph. Lieutenant Harrison. How splendid." Cries of approval rose from Mr. Cable, who stood by his chair at the head of the table and applauded. He'd swapped his blue polo shirt and beige slacks for a gray pinstripe suit. "Well done, Mrs. Hill. They're absolutely perfect. Aren't they, Bill?"

"Divine. You two stay right where you are." The squat balding man in a white long-sleeved shirt, red bow tie, and black tuxedo pants, scrambled to his feet. The expensive tux jacket hung over the back of his chair. A camera with a pricey lens swung by a strap around his neck. He took it in hand. "I'll get some pictures."

"Just smile, or whatever he wants," Lorna whispered to Hart, wondering if the avid photographer would capture any ghosts in the background.

"I shall be most amiable."

If nerves jangled in his gut, he didn't let on. His hands remained warm and steady. But he'd have to be unsure, considering he'd never seen a camera, let alone posed for one under these intimidating circumstances.

Neither had she, for that matter. Modeling wasn't in her job description.

Bill O'Neill bobbed around the room to gauge the best angles. His shiny head popped up here and there, a smidge startling. Clicks sounded and lights flashed as he motioned for them to turn to either side. Darting forward, he adjusted their stance. "Now, gaze up at him as if he's the sun, moon, and stars to you," he instructed Lorna. "And Lieutenant, return that look to this lovely young lady."

"Easily." Hart flooded Lorna with a melting wash of adoration.

If she hadn't witnessed his utter sincerity earlier, she'd wonder at his being a consummate actor. As it was, she *believed*. A wave of heat flowed through her, and she poured her very soul into the look she gave him.

Could such depth of emotion act as a force field and shield them from harm? Especially Hart. She prayed so.

"Excellent pair. They're naturals, John," Bill pronounced.

Mrs. H. snorted. "They're not putting anything on."

Lorna was only distantly aware of her exclamation, and Bill's instructions for 'Lieutenant Harrison to *slowly* escort Miss Randolph to the table.' Yet more pics, she assumed.

A movement behind them caught her notice. Hart turned with her and bowed at the elegant older woman entering the room on the arm of her plain middle-aged assistant. She also used a gold-top cane for support, her ankle-length gown a sheen of silver. Diamond bracelets, rings, and a matching necklace glittered in the light. Her white hair was arranged on her head with a bejeweled tortoiseshell comb tucked in the coils. She'd gone all out for the evening's festivities.

Blue eyes sparkling, she nodded at the assembly. "Sorry we're late. Hazel couldn't speed me along any faster."

Mr. Cable beamed his forgiveness. "That's quite all right. Bill's just getting some shots of our superstars."

"Oh. I see." She turned her piercing gaze on the couple, enveloping them in the magnetism surrounding her like a celestial cloud.

What a remarkable woman. Lorna was glad she'd dressed for the occasion, or that Mrs. Hill had seen to her preparations with the regal lady now scrutinizing her from wig-to-toe. She shifted her regard between them, equally scoping out Hart. Admiration mingled with the wonder shining in her eyes.

"My, oh my. Miss Lorna Randolph and Lieutenant Hart Harrison."

"Yes, ma'am." Lorna wasn't certain which generation of Randolph's and Harrison's she referred to, and had the sense she meant the distant one. "You must be Lady Jane," she said, and clapped a hand over her mouth at the gaffe.

A smile curved Mrs. Randolph's thin, reddened lips and creased her rouged cheeks. "Yes. And don't call me anything else. I prefer the title. Isn't that right, Hazel?" she prompted her quiet companion.

The woman called Hazel nodded. Graying hair twisted into a bun and a fawn dress did nothing to add color to her bland features. But kindness warmed brown eyes muted by shyness.

"They think I don't know about the title." Mrs. Randolph winked at the red-faced Mrs. H. and returned her focus to Lorna and Hart. "I want to sit close enough to both of you to hear every single word."

"Certainly." Mr. Cable hastened to assist his formidable aunt to the table and took one arm while Hazel had the other.

Bill O'Neill hovered nearby in the event his aid was required, and the fake Theo wore an expression of willingness to be of gentlemanly assistance. *Actor*.

"This really is too much. I shall fall over my cane," Lady Jane protested. "Hazel, go sit by Mrs. Hill and leave me to my nephew. I have this handsome officer at my side if need be." She smiled at Hart. "I may be old, but I'm not blind."

Lorna liked her already.

She motioned at the photographer. "Bill might be interested in the couple we passed in the hall. Quite the pair. A Mr. and Mrs. Dare."

Mr. Cable startled. "In my employ?"

Hart tensed beside Lorna, and she inhaled sharply. "No, sir."

The older woman turned farseeing eyes on them. "I don't believe the Dare's would show up well in film."

Neither did Lorna. "Probably not."

"Are they still out there? I could try and get a shot." For a portly man, Bill moved at a fast clip out the door.

Mr. Cable shifted his gaze between his departing friend and his aunt. "Did you speak with the Dares?"

"Yes. They inquired about the ball. We're drawing quite the crowd this year, John. Even the dead are returning."

"Perhaps I should go take a look," he suggested. "We can't have God knows who traipsing the hall and possibly the entire house. Would you see to Aunt Jane, Hart?"

"Gladly." He extended his other arm to Mrs. Randolph. "Please allow me to escort two fair ladies to the table."

She willingly accepted his support. "Nice and strong." Her eyes lifted to his in a long searching gaze. "You're not dead," she concluded, in a lowered voice, "but you are the real Hart Harrison, aren't you?"

How she knew, Lorna had no idea. And she accepted this rather unusual circumstance without evident shock, almost as if she'd been expecting him.

He gave a slight nod. "I am."

If anyone overheard, he could always say he was

playing the part of reenactor. Of course, he'd claim to be himself.

Lady Jane fixed her wise gaze on Lorna. "And you, my dear, are closely knit to the young lady in the portrait." She waved her cane at the wall. "There."

Lorna shifted her focus to the painting at the opposite end of the room she hadn't yet surveyed. The resemblance to the girl she'd beheld in the mirror less than an hour ago was uncanny. Prickles darted through her. If she weren't wearing a wig, her hair might stand on end. She already knew, theoretically, she was linked to the first Lorna—some of her language and mannerisms were sneaking back in—but to see the evidence was staggering.

"Yes. I am," she managed, between gaping lips.

If possible, their regal companion brightened even more. "Well, I must say, I shall have two most remarkable dinner companions this evening."

"I dare say you shall," Hart affirmed. "Though what will pass between us, I cannot surmise."

"Begin by introducing me to that swarthy gentleman eager to be of assistance. Pirate, is he?" she murmured.

Lorna laughed. She'd found a kindred spirit in this woman. "Lady Jane Randolph, this is Sam Brady, an actor and friend of Bill O'Neill's, playing the part of Theo Archer in your nephew's upcoming historical production."

The fake Theo inclined his wigged head. "Pleased to make your acquaintance, ma'am."

"And yours, Mr. Brady." She dismissed him with a glance and returned her attention to Hart. "He doesn't favor Theo Archer in the slightest," she continued in hushed tones.

"No," Hart agreed.

"Not that it matters, really. Visitors don't know the difference," she added.

Lorna considered. "How are you familiar with Theo's appearance, Lady Jane? Is there a portrait of him somewhere?"

"None I'm aware of. I'm basing my impression on the stories that have passed down in the family."

"The Randolphs?" Lorna pressed. "I've heard nothing of him or the duel in our branch."

"No, dear. The Harrison's. Didn't you realize?"

Lorna shook her head.

Hart stared at the older woman. "From whom do you descend in the Harrison family, ma'am, if you have no objection to my inquiring?"

"Not at all. My great-great-great-great grandmother was Adelaide Harrison. Your sister, Lieutenant."

He went a little white. "I gather Adelaide passed along quite a tale."

The farsighted woman nodded. "Jumbled a bit over the years. I remember fragments. Theo Archer was fair-skinned and flaxen haired. Like..." Her complexion paled under the rouge. "That young man coming through the door."

Mr. Cable huffed at the side of the newcomer. "I couldn't find any couple named Dare. But I came across this fellow who claims to be Theo Archer. Did someone hire a second actor?"

Mrs. H. leaned back in her chair, arms folded over her chest. "I certainly didn't. What do we need with two?"

A frostiness came over Hart. "Not a thing."

He lifted his chin and looked down his nose at the slim, fashionably dressed figure in an olive green eighteenth century suit. The dude wore his blond hair pulled back at the neck with a ribbon, a froth of lace at his throat and cuffs, gleaming buckles on his shoes. Kind of a dandy, minus the wig.

"Perhaps this gentleman would be so good as to account for his presence?" Hart said in clipped accents.

Either he'd taken an instant dislike to a lost reenactor, or this was the man whose demise Lorna desired. She studied the admittedly attractive, even boyish face. His puzzled green eyes met hers tinged with disbelief. She unleashed the full force of her gaze, further discomfiting him.

Oh, yeah. He knew who she was. It was times like this she wished she had super powers. The way this guy shrank from her, she kind of did.

He glanced around in apparent confusion, bowing at everyone in the get-together so as not to miss a soul. "I pray you forgive my unannounced presence in your midst. I cannot say how I came to be here without an invitation. But I am acquainted with this lady…" He shifted his incredulous gaze from Lorna to Hart. "And Lieutenant Harrison."

Bill O'Neill puffed in, mopping his head with a handkerchief. "The Dares escaped me." He gaped at the new arrival. "Who the Billy Bob is this?"

Mr. Cable thumbed at the stranger. "Says he's Archer."

"What? Another Theo?" Bill peered at the dude standing a head taller than himself, though shorter than Hart and Mr. Cable. "Sure looks the part. Is word getting out about our production?" He rounded on the stranger. "Who told you about the role?"

Lady Jane interrupted his stuttering reply by tapping her cane on the floor. "I did. Now, come to the table, Mr. Archer, and sit next to Lieutenant Harrison, Miss Randolph, and myself."

Hart's steely gaze pinned the new Theo like a bug. He was no actor but the real deal. Why had Lady Jane covered for him? To gain more information from their baffled guest? They had the advantage over him now, while he was taken off guard. When would the murderous Theo of legend emerge?

Lorna supposed poisoning him would be too much to ask of Cook Betty or her assistant, and Hart running him through at supper might be considered impolite. Besides, he'd set the rules of engagement: No killing anyone not in their own era, or something like that. But the look he leveled at Theo would freeze most men to the bone.

Lord only knew how the new arrival had crossed from the past to the present. The house must've brought him. Why convey their soon-to-be enemy to them?

Clearly, Theo was astonished to find Lorna among the living. Maybe he wondered if he'd joined her in the afterlife. Did he think he'd gone to heaven or hell?

Knowing he was on the verge of challenging Hart to a deadly duel made her want to creep him out all the more. She battled the undignified urge to say 'Boo!' at him. Or mime like a white-faced clown.

Better. She could do her robotic zombie impression. A hit at school. He'd freak.

Catching Theo's furtive gaze on her, she tilted her head stiffly from side-to-side with a pasted glassy expression. His eyes widened.

Hart gave her a look, as if to say, 'Seriously?'

"Shall we proceed, ladies?" Exhibiting extreme self-control, he ignored his would-be nemesis and escorted both women the remainder of the way to the supper table.

He seated Lady Jane at the opposite end from her nephew so that they faced each other across the rectangular length. Each commanded either head of the table, rather like co-captains of an odd vessel with a strange crew aboard.

"By me, Miss Randolph." Lady Jane waved Lorna to her right. Hart helped her into the chair, and she settled with much arranging of skirts. "Sit on my left, Lieutenant, and you, sir, take the seat beside Miss Randolph," their hostess directed, smiling slightly as she gestured at the rattled Theo. He sat where she dictated, ramrod straight in his chair.

He'd fare better beside Hart. The dude was going down under Lorna's watch. If creepy worked, she could do creepy. Maybe he'd run for his life and disappear into time, far away from them. And they'd be free of him and the curse he carried.

Summoning her sweetest glazed-eyed smile, she turned to her dinner companion. "I do hope they serve jellied brains. My favorite," she added, with a robotic head tilt.

Theo's jaw dropped, and he stared, unblinking, at her.

Lady Jane giggled, then laughed. She dabbed the corners of her eyes with a napkin. "You poor sod," she said to the unnerved young man. "Miss Randolph's gunning for you."

The lace knotted at his throat disguised the gulping

swallow. "Why would that be, ma'am?"

She threw her bejeweled hand up. "Oh, you know how it is with the undead. They can be frightfully hungry, but if we keep her well fed, she might not eat you."

Theo appeared ready to bolt, startling in added alarm when Mr. Cable threw back his head and roared. "Aunt, you beat all. And Lorna's a hoot."

Bill broke up, pounding the table in his dissolution. "I love it. Too bad we're not doing a comedy. Eat him—" he choked out, strangled by laughter.

Mrs. H. shook her head, grudging humor in her eyes and the turn of her lips. Mousy Hazel squeaked in amusement.

Sam Brady chuckled, and grunted. "Better him than me."

Hart considered Lorna with a 'Where do I begin' arch in his brow, and a hint of mirth at his mouth. "Oh, I dare say the lady could take both of you gentlemen to task."

She intended to do whatever was necessary to save him.

Chapter Eleven

Exuding enthusiasm, Mr. Cable gestured at his dinner companions seated around the table. "Here's a thought. What if Aunt Jane's candidate auditions for the part of Theo Archer? Seems only fair to allow him the opportunity."

Bill O'Neill shrugged. Willingness to give it a try shaped his chubby face. Sam Brady shot the upstart an 'I'm gonna kill you in your sleep' kind of look but gave their host an obligatory nod. Lady Jane followed the exchange with the alacrity of a raptor tracking prey. She hadn't yet enlightened her nephew as to Theo's true identity.

Why that was, Lorna didn't know, and almost choked on her soda at Mr. Cable's suggestion. She met Hart's tight-lipped stare. He didn't appear overly thrilled at the idea of the Theo parked by her side portraying himself.

That would make three originals in the production. *Freaking bizarre*.

"And," Father John continued. "If Theo number two persuades us he's right for the role, then Sam Brady could take the part of Eli Carter, fellow dragoon and friend of Lieutenant Harrison. Carter acted as the second for him in the duel."

Hart swiveled his head at him. "Do you mean Sergeant *Lee* Carter?"

In a flustered flurry, Mr. Cable dropped his gaze to the notecards scattered beside his half-eaten plate of pot roast. He rifled through them, starring his find with a pen. "Sorry. Yes. Eli was Theo Archer's second, and his last name was Turner. It gets confusing."

He had no idea just how mixed up the whole thing was. Lorna shifted her attention to the newcomer regarding the assembly as if he'd landed on a foreign planet among bloodsucking aliens. Hardly the kind to pick a fight with Hart. More of a wimp than a war lord. She was actually beginning to feel sorry for him.

Was it possible the annals had the wrong guy, or had she missed something?

Catching her focus on him, he shrank back in his chair.

She supposed it was disconcerting to dine beside a lady you assumed was in her grave. "Don't worry," she whispered. "I'm not really undead."

He studied her narrowly. "What are you?" he asked under his breath.

"Reborn." She gestured at the elegant, not completely accurate, period dining room. Discreet modern lighting lent radiance to the glow of candles, and Bill was displaying recent pics in a laptop slide show on a side table.

Hart's baffled gaze frequently roamed there, and he'd had an explanation. She couldn't imagine what Theo must think.

"Haven't you figured it out yet?" She jiggled her glass, clinking perfect cubes. "The ice is a giveaway for a start. You've traveled to the future."

The furrow between his eyes deepened. "How?"

"God knows. The house brought you forward. Sent

Lieutenant Harrison, too."

"Why?"

She tipped another gingery swallow into her mouth and set her chilled glass aside. "Hart, because of me. As for you, you're the conniving devil who killed him in a duel."

For a gaping moment, no words escaped the flabbergasted young man. Then he raised a subtle finger at Hart. "He's seated right there, quite alive."

"Duh," she tossed back, a retort for his ears only, hoping Hart didn't overhear. His eyes already fired warning at this whispered exchange. "The duel hasn't taken place yet in your time."

"Are you a lunatic? Is everyone in this room stark raving mad? That makes no earthly sense." Hissing protest poured from Theo. "Why would I challenge him? He's better at everything than I. Fencing, shooting, riding…his rapid rise to the rank of lieutenant, while I was confined to my bed with fever." He pointed at his left leg. "It left me with a bit of a limp. And all the while, the dashing Hart Harrison excels."

"And how does that make you feel?" she asked, using the well-worn line she'd picked up from psychologists on TV.

He arched his brow at her as if addressing a simpleton. "Envious. Though not foolish enough to challenge him."

She weighed this reasonable response. "Will you be screwing up your courage in a week or two?"

"Courage has no bearing on the matter. Does Lieutenant Harrison intend to impugn my honor?"

"Doubtful," she mused, fiddling with a fake curl

and wondering what it was with men and their honor. "Until today, I doubt he was interested in you one way or the other. You weren't even a blip on his radar."

Theo's lips moved silently as he repeated her assertion, trying to interpret her strange lingo. "His what?"

"Never mind. Do you intend to cross swords with him?"

He exhaled impatiently. "I have no such intention. Have I not said?"

"You have. But history says differently. I have a second question. How about challenging him in pretense, in a play?"

A glimmer of understanding registered with her perplexed companion. "Is that what our host, Mr. Cable, is asking?"

"Yes. He wants you to playact the role of Theo Archer, the murderous duelist."

A flash lit the green depths of his gaze like lightning in a forest. "And besmirch my own name?"

"It is a bit of a stretch," she agreed.

He pursed his mouth, then parted it. "I should like to return to my home now."

She lifted one rustling shoulder and let it drop. "Fine by me. If we've reached an accord on the whole *you don't want to challenge Hart Harrison thing*."

"I fail to see how such action is to my advantage."

"Nor do I. Glad I've persuaded you of the folly of such a course."

Scorn curved his youthful good looks, the sort of male beauty that landed you roles in plays like Mr. Cable's, or movies. Theo was a shoo-in for the part of pretty boy Frank Churchill in the next production of

Jane Austen's *Emma*, or Dorian in *The Picture of Dorian Gray*.

"You persuaded me of nothing. I never intended this act." The arms crossed over his chest stance indicated Theo's resolve, and mounting annoyance.

A thought occurred to her. "If you have no grievance with Lieutenant Harrison, why were you in this house in the middle of the night?"

"How do you know it was the middle of the night?" he countered. "'Tisn't now."

"The hour there doesn't necessarily coincide with the hour here. Hart popped back not long ago and found the household abed and the clock striking two in the morning."

"Nonsense. This going back and forth like a cork in and out of a bottle is insane. I shall awake and find the whole matter a bizarre dream."

"I hope you do. Soon." The dude was getting on her nerves. He had a peevish quality about him. *Whiney baby* was another term for it. She hadn't noted the limp.

Theo prodded her shoulder with his index finger. "I shall recall you, Miss Randolph, as the strangest of all. Undead enchantress."

She grabbed his finger and bent it back, resulting in an audible gasp. "Touch me again and I'll break it." Catfights with three sisters had taught her well.

He snatched his hand away, eyeing her with incredulity. "You, miss, are no lady."

"Hurling insults at me will do you no good service, sir," she countered icily, in the language of the first Lorna. "Nor does it explain your presence here in the wee hours."

He glared at her. "If you must know, I was caught

in a storm, and Mrs. Harrison invited me to stay the night. The good woman is mindful of my health."

"Bravo for her. But why were you here in the first place?" Lorna repeated.

"I called on Adelaide Harrison."

Now they had trouble. She couldn't imagine the bubbly brilliant young woman settling for any man less sterling than her adored brother.

Still laughing at some witticism of Bill's, Lady Jane turned toward Lorna. "What are you two buzzing about over here?"

"Nothing. And everything." She leaned closer to speak near the older woman's ear. "Is Theo related to you?"

Mirth faded, and the innate wisdom she emanated returned to her demeanor. "Not remotely."

"So he isn't your ancestor?" Lorna pressed in a whisper.

"No. And I understand what you're getting at. He doesn't wed Adelaide."

"Who doesn't?" Hart's hawk ears must've detected her name in the flow.

Lorna nodded at Theo, glowering in pregnant silence.

A red hue flushed Hart's face. "I should hope not. She has an understanding with Lee Carter. Not yet announced. Even so." He rounded on the usurper. "You dare court my sister? You are deficient in every single quality she deserves."

Mr. Cable pounced. "Great intro line for the source of contention between you two." He jotted busily on his card.

Was he actually taking notes? Hart appeared ready

to jerk Theo out of his chair and throw him against the wall.

The source of all this contention smirked at Lorna from his seat. "Deficient, am I? History says I win the duel."

A spasm skewered her, and anger turned up the heat. "That was before."

"What?" he challenged.

"The undead enchantress, as you termed me." She thrust her face nearer his. "What do you suppose I might do to you, you sniveling worm? Cast a spell? Turn you into a toad."

Theo drew back, his eyes wide green pools.

"Excellent conflict! Keep it coming—" Mr. Cable caught himself. "Wait. You're not part of the duel."

"I am now." She reached for her drawstring purse.

Hart grasped her shoulder. "Enough."

She hadn't noticed him spring from his seat and dash to her. "Oh, I'm just getting started."

"Leave the pistol in your reticule," he ordered.

Theo gaped at her. "You would shoot me?"

"Sure would, then toss you back in time. And you *lose*."

Applause. "Oh, she's marvelous, John," Bill called between resounding claps. "Such depth. We need more scope for her talent. After this production, we should do Shakespeare. Can't you just picture her in *The Taming of the Shrew*?"

"I can. And *Annie Get Your Gun*." He chortled at his wit.

Theo straightened in his seat. "She's acting?"

"What did you think? She'd really blow your brains out?" Mr. Cable doubled over in mirth. "Oh my,

Lorna. You are fearsome."

Laughter ripped from everyone except Hart, who did not appear in the least amused, and Theo, who wore a peevish expression. Lady Jane tittered politely, her telescopic gaze scanning the three originals. She must have had some kind of special eye surgery and lenses implanted because nothing escaped her notice, even at her age.

Bill blotted his streaming face with his handkerchief. "The first Lorna Randolph was very sweet, I'm sure, but more like arm candy for Lieutenant Harrison." He swept his hand at Lorna. "This fiery young lady would have fought the British herself."

"No need," Mr. Cable inserted between bouts of hilarity. "The officers would have fallen for her in droves. Her home wouldn't have been among those burned."

Hart gripped the back of Lorna's seat and bent toward him. "When?"

Father John appeared surprised. It took him a moment to gain control over his merriment. "Oh, right. Not in your memory bank. The Brits attacked Virginia in early January seventeen eighty-one. They sacked Richmond, then looted and burned homes along the James. Berkeley Plantation, for one. Plundered, not burned."

He paled. "Harrison Hall?"

"No. They left here in a hurry. It's a mystery, really."

"Maybe the ghosts scared them off," Lady Jane suggested.

Her nephew swung into pensive mode, as if the idea of a paranormal deterrent had merit. "Maybe.

Likely there's a story in here somewhere."

Theo hung on their every word. "What of the Turner place where I reside with my aunt and uncle?"

"Tell them to batten down the hatches and hide the silver before the British invasion."

Bill gestured at Lorna. "Speaking of a fight. Show us this pistol of yours."

She lifted her weighty purse and took out the replica of a ladies' revolver. She aimed it at Theo. "Bang."

After his initial flinch, he bared his teeth in an ingratiating smile.

Sam Brady grinned, his artificially whitened teeth and snowy wig blinding. "She held me hostage with that earlier this evening. She's a very convincing actress, I must say."

Mr. Cable still wore his thoughtful face. "Yes, we're blessed in her coming to us. We'll have to see what more we can do to increase her role in this production, and bear other opportunities in mind down the road. What say you, Lieutenant? Are you impressed by your co-star? Not to take away from your own ability, of course. You are most impressive."

Hart gave a bow. "Thank you, sir. I am indeed awed by Miss Randolph. She exceeds my *every* expectation."

The way he said it made her think that wasn't entirely a good thing.

"As for you, our new Theo. Well done." Mr. Cable applauded him. "Your rendition of spoiled Virginia gentry was superb. I can safely say the part is yours."

The uncertainty in Theo's expression was rewarding to behold. "I, um, thank you for your gracious—Wait, spoiled?"

Their would-be director interrupted his sputtering. "I assume you will remain with us?"

He halted in mid-stutter. "Here? At Harrison Hall?"

"We can't push for a play in a few weeks without all hands on deck twenty-four seven. Mrs. Hill will find you a spot."

She appeared accustomed to these sudden demands. "No one's in the trailer right now. It's snug but has air-conditioning and a bathroom," she added, in the event Theo was worried for his creature comforts. "Stow your gear in there."

He digested this. "What gear would that be, ma'am?"

She rolled her eyes. "Not another one? Never mind. We're acquiring supplies for unequipped reenactors. I suppose you will insist on being called Theo Archer at all times?"

He spread his palms. "Mister, or sir, will also serve."

Hart snorted. "He isn't qualified for any other title."

Balling his hands into fists, Theo hurled, "I shall be."

"What? Your lordship?" Hart tossed back.

"Now, now, gentlemen," Lady Jane hushed them. "Save it for the play."

What was her game, anyway? Why conceal Theo's true identity? And why cover for Lorna and Hart? They had only succeeded in further antagonizing their mortal enemy. But she supposed if the house intended to deposit Theo in the present indefinitely, he couldn't do any harm in the past. Maybe the best way to prevent the conniving worm from fulfilling his vile destiny was to keep him here, and a sharp eye out. They'd have to watch each other's backs.

This was gonna be one hell of a production.

Mr. Cable surveyed them happily. "To think I began this day without any notion of producing an event of such magnitude, and none of my cast present. Now, here you are. My golden ones." His fond gaze lingered on Lorna and Hart, brushing Theo in passing. "You came, and I'm overwhelmed. What can I say?"

She was speechless herself. A glance at Hart suggested he had plenty to say, was positively brimming over. If he expected her not to defend herself, or dive-bomb potential assaults on his security, he had another thing coming.

Lorna number one was dead. Long live Lorna number two. And long live Hart. Even if he was pissed.

Chapter Twelve

Like black lace, moonbeams filtered the leaves fluttering beyond the parlor windows and shone through the old beveled glass. Candelabras burned white-gold, scenting the evening with beeswax. The thick cord sectioning off the room had been laid aside, freeing the space for their gathering.

The harpsichord gifted by George Washington and restored by Mr. Cable came to life under his proficient fingers. The formerly mousy Hazel, unrecognizable as master of the violin, stood at Father John's side. Head and bun thrown back, she slid her bow over the strings, unleashing a melodious stream. Music filled the room as it might have nearly two and a half centuries ago. Would ghosts pirouette to such invitation?

Anything might happen, Lorna considered, seated next to Hart on the gold couch. His highly distracting presence sent ribbons of heat up her side and through her middle. Despite the thrill of his closeness, she wondered when she'd hear about her behavior at supper. He hadn't said a word. Yet.

While they posed together, Bill bobbed around, snapping photographs. Mrs. H. and Lady Jane looked on from armchairs before the hearth. Candles flickering overhead on the mantel and small tables nearby played over their faces. Sam Brady positioned a high-backed Queen Anne chair beside the women and joined them.

Laughter punctuated the gathering as he regaled them with stories. They might not be young and beautiful, but that didn't dissuade him from making a meal of their attention.

"What a merry party. Mr. Brady is nothing if not charming," Hart muttered, clearly not a fan. "No doubt, he realizes Lady Jane is a potential patron."

"Indeed. Will you scold me and get it over with?" Lorna twisted the drawstring on her purse. "The suspense is unbearable."

His lips curved slightly. "Just punishment then." With a sigh, he shook his head at her. "Would it make any difference if I did berate you?"

"Not a lot," she admitted.

"Would you believe strong men quake at my words?"

"Yes and no. Depends on which Hart they're dealing with."

"Not this one, I assure you."

"Cozy up, guys." The genial photographer gestured the couple nearer together.

"I make no objection." Hart closed his arm around Lorna, and she smiled up at him, teasing a shade of laughter in eyes more blue than gray.

He angled his mouth near her ear. "What do you remember from before?"

Nostalgia tugged at her. A strong sense of the past and present merged in the parlor. Her former self may have died upstairs in the bedchamber, but her story unfolded down here.

She answered beneath the soulful melody. "This room."

"Yes. You loved it here. The music and

dancing…"

"Funny, I don't recall a step."

"You will."

"Your assurance is heartening, sir. At least we made it across the hall without exiting the century. But we're stuck with you know who." She nodded at Theo, poised near the door. "Watching for his escape. Wish we could give him a shove."

"After the house transported him forward, it seemingly eased off the continual ebb and flow in time," Hart observed.

"Yeah. Stranding him with us. You realize he probably visited the parlor earlier this evening in the company of the fair Adelaide—in seventeen seventy-seven."

Tension was palpable in Hart at the mention of his sister coupled with Theo. "Being inexplicably torn from her may account for his perpetual expression of peevish bemusement."

"Which casts gloom over all. Can't we send him back?"

Hart frowned, something he'd done a lot this evening. "We dare not reveal the portal. Guard that secret with your life."

"Right." Adelaide, alone, knew of the connection between the past and present in the bathroom/closet beneath the stairs. "I guess we're stuck with Theo indefinitely."

"Until the duel, I suspect."

The somber reminder, in his low tone, weighted Lorna like a stone. "I will prevent your end. Somehow. I swear it."

Admiration hinted in his gaze. "If there is any way

possible, you will find it. Yet all does not depend on you."

Her gut begged to differ. "Deep down, I feel it does."

"I have a part to play." He smoothed her cheek, sending quivers through her. "Take heart, my brave miss. We are here, not there. And Mr. Archer isn't currently hell-bent on my destruction."

"*Mutual* destruction," she emphasized. "I assured him of that end, should he be foolish enough to proceed."

"I have every confidence he will rue the day." A smile touched Hart's eyes, swiftly replaced by furrowed contemplation. "I still do not understand why the annals say he challenged me. Granted, his temper is short. But he's not foolhardy and only has a slight chance of winning, as he well knows. If it were merely a point of honor, we would both fire our pistols in the air and be done with it. Given the choice, though, I will choose swords, which he also knows, and battle to first blood. This challenge strikes me more as the act of his cousin, Eli Turner, the man Mr. Cable named as his second in the duel."

She strove to think. "I wish I could remember Eli. You recall Mr. Cable said there were accusations of cheating?"

Hart's jaw tightened. "If the two colluded together, perhaps that brought them success."

An icy chill pierced her. "It brought Theo the contempt of his neighbors and drove him to New York."

"Far from his doting aunt and uncle." Hart rubbed his freshly shaven chin between his thumb and forefinger. "The question remains, what happened to Eli Turner?"

"That could be essential. We should make inquiries—"

Bill beckoned, interrupting their hushed conversation. "Let's get you two circling on the floor."

She gulped. "Dancing?"

He beamed at them over his camera lens. "Nothing more romantic."

A new fear loomed. She gripped Hart's arm.

"Do not distress yourself," he soothed, getting to his feet and drawing her up with him. "I shall guide you. Leave your reticule with the fake pistol on the couch. And cease making faces at Theo."

"Spoilsport."

A wry smile curved his lips. "Plaguing the fellow does no good. Nor does aiming that foolish pistol."

"Not so foolish if it's believable," she argued.

"Only to the untutored eye."

"There's a lot of that about this evening."

Muffling his laughter, he nodded. "You have frightened the life out of two gentlemen."

"I'm very scary."

"No. You're not. Only in how I fear for you. Though you are far better able to defend yourself than you once were."

A warm glow suffused her at his admission.

Bill waved them forward. "A dance, John and Hazel," he called to the rapt musicians. "Nothing too spritely. Think romance, not jigs."

The two paused to confer over their choice and turned pages covered with notes.

"I realize you can't perform an eighteenth century

dance by yourselves. It wants couples," Bill allowed. "A shame waltzing wasn't commonplace yet. Just do the best you can. The lighting's fabulous this evening, you're both divine, and close shots will work for the pics."

At a signal from Hart, their accompanists struck up a slower melody than the livelier English country dances required. Its poignant beauty throbbed with romance. Lorna's heart fluttered as he led her to the center of the room and stood facing her. She was acutely aware of being the focus of attention and didn't care for either Sam or Theo's expressions. The latter had abandoned his post by the door and seated himself with the others. Envy was plain in the men.

"Eyes on me," Hart directed, scowling at the two males.

Bill's laugh boomed. "Don't fret gents, plenty of partners tomorrow. We're bringing in a dance troupe, so I trust you know your steps."

Theo sneered. "I have received instruction in dance since the age of twelve."

Not Lorna. She envisioned a packed room, overflowing into the hall, and her middle knotted. "How will I ever keep up?"

"Follow me." Hart smiled reassuringly and bowed. She returned the formality.

He stepped forward, lightly circled his arm around her waist and turned with her, then stepped back. Again, he closed the distance between them, circling around her, brushed her hand, and spun away. His graceful turns, lowering and raising of his shoulders and dipping at the waist were pure elegance.

An innate knowledge came to her aid, the sort that

guides migrating birds. She didn't falter as badly as she'd feared, but she lacked his grace. Practice would help her mimic his dip and flow.

Clasping her fingers, he turned again with her. "We did dance alone," he said, in a voice only she could hear.

"What dance?"

"The waltz or *walzer*, though not so anyone knew."

She nodded. "I thought so. But the waltz wasn't common?"

"'Twas in Germany and Vienna." He took her hand, closing his other arm around her back, eliciting near electric sparks at his touch. "I wanted a special dance for us and had an instructor come to the house in secret. A portly enthusiastic German man, rather like Mr. O'Neill." He angled his tall figure so they revolved shoulder to shoulder, or as near as she could come to it, gazing into each other's eyes. "We waltzed in the garden by moonlight."

Shadowed memories swirled in her mind. "Through the boxwood hedges?"

"Yes." His answering smile stole her breath.

For a long moment, they slowly revolved to the music.

His eyes glistened. "Make no mistake, I loved that Lorna with my whole being."

Her heart caught. "And this one?"

"I am acquiring a taste for her."

"Only a taste?"

A smile flickered. "Are you jealous of yourself?"

"In the strangest possible way, yes. If you could choose, which Lorna would you pick?" She envisioned them side-by-side.

"They are one and the same," he insisted.

"We both know they're not." She whirled away.

He caught her hand and spun her back toward him. "You, it's always you."

"I pray so. My choice was made centuries ago." Both Lornas were all about him, and that wasn't going to change. Ever. If she lost him, her heart would be torn out.

"Whoever you are, you're still my Lorna." His words in her ear, he led her across the room.

"With a few alterations."

He darted a smile at her. "More than a few."

"And likely to be still more."

"Doubtless." He glided with her in spirals.

"I'm relieved you are accepting."

"Intrigued, wary, apprehensive…all better describe my mood. Have care you do not endanger us both."

His warning set off alarm bells. Care wasn't a commodity she had a great deal of when it came to this duel.

Turning on her toes, she stepped forward to meet him. "I will be more careful."

Laughter from the group by the hearth muffled her assertion. "You will *mean* to be," Hart emphasized. "And yet forge ahead with anyone you perceive as a threat."

Indignation swelled in her. "What would you have me do?"

"Keep your eyes and ears open, and *remember*."

"But I wasn't alive when the duel took place."

"No. Yet you were before it. Something may occur to you."

She nodded, willing herself to recall any useful

141

Beth Trissel

detail from her shrouded, extremely distant past.

"And," he continued softly, "help me ferret out anything of significance regarding the key players."

"You make them sound like actors in a play."

He swirled around with her. "They are. We all are."

"True," she fully realized. "We're to reenact the very event."

"But the theater is quite real," he added gravely.

Pushing aside grim awareness, she clung to this moment...the moonbeams filtering through the windows, the revolving room in its candlelit splendor, the spice in Hart's cologne, and most vital of all, to him. His precious warmth pressed against her meant he was alive, and she intended for him to remain that way.

Chapter Thirteen

Evening practice on the lawn at Harrison Hall

"My angel!" Father John called to Lorna, rather like the Phantom to Christine in *Phantom of the Opera,* and applauded her in the middle of her song.

The engrossed director/composer was prone to these outbursts, and the string ensemble accompanying her carried on. The not-so-mousy Hazel, when in command of her violin, was well accustomed to his eccentricities. She didn't bat an eye.

Lorna didn't miss a note. Her voice soared heavenward among the leafy boughs arching above them. The dramatic aria, pulsing with emotion, reminded her of *Abigail's Song* in *Doctor Who.* Not exactly colonial.

Mr. Cable justified his departure from historically accurate pieces by citing the Broadway hit *Hamilton,* which he loved. He wasn't into hip-hop music, but his original compositions were prominent in this production, and none suited the era they were depicting. He'd given Lorna several solos, Hart and Theo each had one. She and Hart sang a duet. Fortunately, he and Theo didn't. Father John had even engaged a choir for the grand finale.

When she wasn't singing, she was dancing with Hart, the troupe, and other cast members, including

Sam and Theo. No departures here. Mr. Cable stuck to period dances.

Inhaling the vanilla scent of white magnolia blossoms, she scanned the cast clustered in corners of the yard between bright flower beds. Mr. Cable, the camera-ready Bill O'Neil, and her accompanists, including Hazel, sat in chairs behind the stage. Lorna stood in the center of the wooden platform, wigless, her hair pinned up beneath a wide straw hat encircled with ribbons attached beneath her chin. A butterfly the hue of her saffron gown fluttered in the light breeze. Late day sunbeams dappled the trees rising around her like sentinels, their thickly furrowed trunks centuries old.

There. She spotted Hart at a distance seated atop the chestnut stallion he'd named Rock for his endurance. When Harrison Hall brought him forward, Rock came with him. Hart, in his blue and red-faced uniform, buff-colored leather breeches, and black riding boots, was smoking hot on the magnificent horse. Mr. Cable had him ditch the dragoon helmet/hat so the audience could better appreciate his killer looks. His glossy brown hair, pulled back at his neck, caught the light.

Her heart hitched each time she saw him. He blew her a kiss, and she nearly lost track of where she was in the song. This one had the highest range, too. If only they had two seconds alone. She wished he'd bound onto the stage and take her in his arms again, as he'd done in an earlier scene.

She'd also welcome his support. Only excitement and fearful anticipation kept her from sagging to the stage floor in exhaustion. Mr. Cable rehearsed the cast in the evenings after guests departed and in the mornings before they arrived. She knew everyone's lines, plus her own. Even recited them in her sleep.

Between practices, she and Hart had dance lessons, were taken on more photo shoots, and greeted the throng ascending on Harrison Hall like the lord and lady of the manor. Days had passed without forays to the past, or visitors from that era brought forward, but their time was not their own. Not yet.

She twirled a green parasol as she sang, prepared to use it as a weapon on Theo, if need be. So far, he'd done what was required of him. Still, her chest tightened at the thought of the actual duel.

Her song trailed off on the last moving note, like the final trill of a lark. Hushed appreciation emanated from the onlookers, then applause broke out. She'd nailed it and had to admit their caffeine-fueled composer was brilliant.

"I've stayed up nights composing," he announced, his voice cracking from fatigue and emotion. "This song is my finest achievement, and Lorna did it proud." He blotted his eyes, blew his nose, and Bill gave him a congratulatory hug.

Hart smiled and tipped his hand to her, the greatest tribute of all.

"Thank you." Swollen with indescribable sentiment, she curtsied and stepped to the back of the platform.

Practice sped past. She noted Theo, and Deb Rivera, the actress playing Adelaide, take their positions on stage. The pretty boy villain wore clothes well, and Mrs. H. had been instructed to spare no expense in attiring him. The tailored suits accentuated his slim agile figure while Deb dazzled in voluminous gowns. Theo's blond head shone in contrast to the auburn curls tumbling around her shoulders.

They were an attractive pair and accompanied the golden couple on some shoots. Lorna suspected Theo liked Deb more than simply as a fellow actor, and she slanted admiring brown eyes at him. Would this alter anything in the past, or was it a mild flirtation, and he was still mad about Adelaide?

He stepped into character—his actual self—and took Deb's hand. "Such a fair evening, Miss Harrison. Made all the more delightful by your lovely presence. Linger a moment with me, sweet lady."

Unlike the high-spirited Adelaide, Deb bowed her head modestly. "I thank you, sir. But you must excuse me. You really must." She attempted to pull her fingers away.

Theo held on. "Give me a chance to win your heart, I beg you. Stroll about the garden with me."

"I pray you release me, sir. I must return to the house."

Hoof beats. The entrapped female glanced around. "Hart!"

He cantered to the stage on his swift mount. No matter how often Lorna saw him ride in, her heart sped along with the horse's outstretched legs.

"Adelaide!" He halted the big stallion and hurled himself from the saddle, thrusting the reins at the stable boy/pressed into actor waiting in readiness. "Cease your attentions to my sister, sir!"

Theo sneered convincingly. "I have every right to court her."

"You have none! As my father would inform you were he here."

"Your dear mother has given her approval."

"Mama is not well!" With the agility of a panther, Hart leapt onto the stage. He tossed his coat to a cast member and stood in his long-sleeved white shirt beneath the red waistcoat with pewter buttons. The leather breeches were molded to his long legs and met his black riding boots.

His magnetism threw everyone else into shadow. "You unworthy ferret!" He lunged at Theo.

The two men grabbled with convincing antagonism. Not hard to muster, considering they loathed each other.

"You dare insult me!" Theo hurled with believable venom. "I demand satisfaction. Name your weapons. Choose the hour and place."

Hart glared at him. "Swords. Here and now."

The actor portraying Theo's cousin, Eli Turner, and Sam Brady, playing Lee Carter, Hart's friend and fellow officer, rushed forward. Why Lee, who supposedly had an understanding with Adelaide and must have been seeking her at the ball, didn't initiate this protest himself, was lost on Lorna. And she and Hart had unearthed nothing noteworthy about Eli.

According to tradition, the ball was underway at sunset on Midsummer Eve when he discovered Theo with Adelaide in the garden and the argument erupted. He wasn't on horseback. Mr. Cable added that dramatic bit. He'd already returned home for a visit.

Sam, the actor playing Lee, retrieved Hart's sword from the house, as the one worn by dragoons in a shoulder harness didn't suit the purpose. In actuality, he had his sword at the time of the duel, and Theo drew his rapier from his side. The two men insisted on using their original blades on stage and vowed caution to a reluctant Mr. Cable. Lorna shivered at the danger, and the playacting of a tragic event, that weirdly, hadn't yet happened. One she was bent on preventing.

She and fake Adelaide/Deb tucked up their skirts and descended the steps to the base of the stage, while remaining close enough to follow every move Hart and Theo made. The seconds kept a close watch on the combatants, and the curious gathered as they would have done those many years ago. Father John looked on from the sidelines, waving his arms like a conductor leading an orchestra, which he also did. From what he'd learned, Theo's pursuit of Adelaide caused the duel. Lady Jane agreed, and Hart glowered at the suggestion, so chances were this is exactly how he had reacted.

Despite Theo's avowal he'd never challenge Hart, his temper must've gotten the better of him. But how did he win? That made no sense.

Hart curved his lips in a smile only a foolish man would disregard. Theo refused to be intimidated and strutted for the cast. No limp in evidence. Claps resounded for the bad boy. Theo was annoyingly popular and perfect for the part.

Heck. He ought to be. He portrayed himself. Even Lorna had to admit he was talented, also at singing and dancing.

"Confound it, Archer!" Hart had scant patience with his preening co-star. He bounded forward with the dexterity of the rider/warrior, slicing his blade at Theo's sword. If this were a deadly duel, he'd slice it at his head or plunge it into his heart.

No. This is a performance, she reminded herself. Plus, Hart said he only fought to first blood, which meant the first injury inflicted, generally a nonfatal wound. And Theo wasn't keen on being stuck in the future in the maximum security prison she'd threatened him with if he lashed out recklessly. He might have gotten away with a deadly duel in the past. Modern times were not so forgiving, she'd warned. Nor was she.

The script called for him to strike back at Hart with a strong downward swoop, which he swiftly dealt. Hart brought his blade up, blocking that blow. He swung higher. The clash of steel rang out again and again.

Hart dodged the rapier coming at him and spun around. He drove Theo back. The 'I dare you' grin he wore transformed his face into a man Lorna had never seen. What else did she not know about him?

If Theo weren't handy with a sword, he'd already have a red stripe down one shoulder. At the very least. He struck hard. Hart side-stepped his swing, tapping him with the flat of his sword in passing. "A hit!" He pivoted and took a bow.

Was that really necessary? Theo was genuinely furious, the rage on his face quite real at being bested. But he couldn't run Hart through, even if he were able to enact the deed, with everyone looking on. Not then, and not now.

Steel whistled through the air as Hart swung the blade over his head. Theo parried that stroke, and the next. The two circled the room eyeing each other, thrusting here and there.

Hart made a fantastic leap, side-stepped the oncoming blade, and spun around. He varied this move each evening, like an improvisational dancer. Theo never saw it coming, and Hart got in another tap with the flat of his sword. Possibly, he'd inflicted a bloody stripe at this moment in the past.

Waving his sword in victory, he strode around the stage. "Shall we call it done? I declare this duel won."

The seconds nodded. Sam Brady appeared genuinely impressed with the star of this production. Everyone whose eye Lorna caught was wowed by Hart.

A tight-faced Theo gave a short bow and darted off the stage, circling around in the dusky light. He exchanged his sword for the retractable dagger Mrs. H., their prop mistress, provided. The blade in hand, he stole behind Hart. As brother and sister spoke together in hushed tones, Theo stabbed his antagonist in the back.

Hart slumped to his knees with a sharp cry that pierced Lorna to her soul. Boos rose from members of the cast also acting as the crowd. Theo disappeared into the gloom like a thief in the night, an act he'd declared his revulsion for, muttering about *dishonor*. He'd argued his accused role in a private hissing session with Lorna. But this might well be how Hart's end took place, how it still might.

And yet, she didn't really believe Theo capable of such deceit. Angry, sulking, trying to leave his mark during the duel, yes. But this? He couldn't win over Hart honorably. That was clear. Had he cheated, or was there something or someone not yet accounted for?

Chapter Fourteen

As zonked as Lorna was from hours of practice, she gradually became aware of someone hovering by her bed. At first, the sensation of being watched melded with her dreams. An aura of intense grief hung over the figure. Then a voice spoke, cracked with pain. The words were garbled.

"My darling girl. I failed you," a woman lamented, more clearly.

What?

"Doctor Pace did no good with his leeches and bleeding," she choked out. "I should have sent for Mama Kay sooner. Her fever nostrums lacked time to work their healing power."

Mama Kay…the name was a familiar echo in the dim tunnel of the past. A face attached itself to the distant form, and a black woman with wise, chocolate-colored eyes took shape in Lorna's hazy recollection. She wore a red scarf knotted around her dark head, gold hoops at her ears, and a cut glass necklace encircling her throat. Her skillful brown fingers dispensed tinctures, slicked on salves, applied poultices…

Yeah. Mama Kay would've been a better choice. Wait. She'd lived in the seventeen hundreds.

Lorna opened drowsy eyes, blinking at the lace-capped profile of Hart's mother, Mrs. Harrison. Moonbeams slanting through the window and the orange glow in the hearth revealed the huddled figure in a chair drawn close to her bedside. She looked like a ghost in her white nightdress and pale shawl, but Lorna couldn't see through her.

The piney aromatic fragrance of herbs steaming in the fireplace scented the room. *Medicinal*, she supposed.

Holy crap. With Midsummer and the production nearly upon them, the house was at it again. Question was, had she gone backward in time, or had Mrs. Harrison been brought forward?

Clue: An herbal-scented fire wasn't crackling in the hearth when she'd dozed off. Second clue: The room was cool and Mrs. Harrison snugly wrapped. Lorna number one had fallen ill and died in the wet chill of spring, not mid-June. The house really had taken her back—to her deathbed.

All this flashed through her rapidly waking mind. *What to do?* She couldn't remain here. She must get to the portal and the future. How to navigate her way past Mrs. Harrison?

Weeping. The distraught woman buried her face in a handkerchief. "Dear Lord. How shall I ever bear to tell Hart? He loves the girl more than his life."

Poor lady. A pang went through Lorna at her stark anguish and fear for Hart. Did she think the girl lying before her to be dead or dying? In her mind, was she keeping vigil with the gravely ill or a corpse? That made a big difference to what might follow.

Uncertain if she'd be of comfort to the despairing soul or just freak her out more, she whispered, "It will be all right, Mrs. Harrison."

She startled and turned toward her. Tears streamed

from her swollen eyes. "You spoke. You are not gone from us?"

"Not yet."

The enlivened woman pressed her hand to Lorna's forehead. "Cooler. Perhaps 'tisn't too late for the fever nostrums."

Now what had she gotten herself into, giving the mourner false hope? How the house had interchanged the two Lorna's, she couldn't fathom, but the first one didn't survive. *Fact.*

She covered the trembling fingers on her brow and lightly squeezed them. "A brief reprieve. Death is soon upon me, dear lady. You cannot prevent it," she murmured in the language of Lorna number one. "Know I bear you no ill will. Only love. This is not the end. We shall meet again. And Hart will find me. I promise."

Her eyes widened into incredulous pools, and her lips quivered. "The Lord be praised, allowing me these precious words from you."

Lorna did the only thing she could under the *unusual* circumstances, smiled faintly, fluttered her eyes shut, and prayed she'd be transferred to the modern-day version of her bedroom. *Take me back.*

Still, Mrs. Harrison bent over her, sniffling and blowing her nose. "Sweet child," she gasped between her tears. "Thank you, God, for this glimpse of our beloved girl."

The swish of skirts indicated another female had entered the room. The hint of jasmine accompanied her. "Mama? Is she gone?" The voice belonged to Adelaide.

"Not quite." Mrs. Harrison sniffed. "She spoke to me."

"I thought her past speech. What did she say?"

"Death will not part us forever."

"No. It will not." Adelaide clasped Lorna's hand. "Perhaps she will speak again. Lorna, have you a farewell for me?"

She'd love to gift her friend with a grateful parting but must remain true to history. What were the first Lorna's final words? Adelaide had told her when the two girls met by the cupboard/bathroom below the stairs.

Not words. *Word.* She opened her eyes, gazing at the pleading faces bent near her. Adelaide's tender regard was so like her brother's, except puffy from weeping. There was only one thing she could say.

"Hart." With his dear name on her lips, she shut her eyes. She'd just enacted Lorna one's death scene.

A swirling mist enfolded her. *What's this?* Was she really dying?

****

When Lorna awoke again, moonbeams streamed a pearly path through the window into her pitch-black room. She jerked to life. Had the fire in the hearth gone out, or was she back in the present?

She inhaled, detecting no herbal fragrance apart from the lavender sachets Mrs. Hill tucked everywhere with near religious fervor. No smoky scent from a wood fire either. As far as she could tell, she was alone. No one stood near. She patted her goose-pimply arms and cotton front to see if she still wore the oversized *Hairy Pawter* cat with glasses t-shirt she'd had on at bedtime.

Yep. Whew. The house had zapped her back to twenty seventeen. But for how long, and what else was about to happen?

Clearly, anything might.

Hart! She scrambled from bed. Not pausing for her pink slipper socks, she ran barefoot across the room. A turn of the knob, and she bolted out the door and into the path of Mr. and Mrs. Dare.

She stopped abruptly, barely muffling a scream. *Crap*! Why did they do that? They'd give her heart failure.

Oblivious to her ravaged nerves, they regarded her with faces pursed in disdain. What did they have to be so stuck-up about? The wall was faintly visible through their meticulously attired forms. She had half a mind to tell them.

Mrs. Dare wrinkled her nose and swept an opaque hand at Lorna's shirt. "What French fashion is this, Miss Randolph?"

Mr. Dare drew a pinch of snuff from his enameled box. "You cannot possibly wear that to the ball, young lady."

Oh hell, she'd play along. "I assure you I shall be decked out like Queen Elizabeth's flag ship on the big eve." They could choose which Elizabeth they assumed she meant. Chilled through by the specters, she pointed shakily down the hall. "Pray return below stairs and await the festivities while the family ready themselves. Refreshments will be served shortly."

"Very well." A short bow, and her ghostly visitors sauntered arm-in-arm out of sight into the mist.

Would they stroll into the hereafter after the ball was concluded? Harrison Hall had gone insane. Who else might it summon forth?

Was that a flicker of light, or a figure she glimpsed over her shoulder? *Cripes*! A servant girl they didn't have skirted down the hall in a white apron. *That's it!* She wasn't hanging around to meet any more unearthly visitors.

She tore at Hart's door. Too freaked to knock, she burst inside gasping like the entire British Legion galloped in pursuit. She'd prefer soldiers to ghosts. Although, they could probably be apparitions, too. As could the horses.

Scratch that.

Chapter Fifteen

Lorna bolted into Hart's room like a runaway horse and found him reclining in bed, propped against the pillows. A candle burned on the nightstand, and he had antiquated leather-bound books piled around him. He held an open volume in his hands.

He turned his head at her, and his eyes widened beneath an arching brow. The book slipped to his lap.

She returned his astonishment. "Seriously? It's like two in the morning, and you're reading?"

Not that he didn't look cool doing it in a colonial-style white shirt revealing a muscular chest patterned with brown hair. No waxing for him…glorious masculinity. Without the cravat knotted at his neck, the shirt hung open in front. The chestnut brown hair he always wore pulled back now hung loose around his shoulders, and his rolled sleeves revealed strong arms. The blanket was loosely drawn over the outline of his lower half.

"I only need a few hours of sleep." He gestured at her. "What on earth are you wearing?"

She figured the first question out of his mouth would be what are you doing here? They weren't in the habit of nightly visits after he'd vowed honorable behavior. "My favorite cat t-shirt." She gestured at the door she'd shut behind her. "I just went through this with the Dare's out in the hall."

He exhaled heavily. "They're back then?"

"Sure are. And before that, I hung out with your mom and sister. Not too cheery. Apparently, I was dying at the time."

His jaw dropped open. "Jesus, Mary, and Joseph. The house returned you to that moment?"

"Sure did. Why don't you just say 'Holy Cow?' And I saw some girl who doesn't belong here run past." Lorna bounded, trembling, over the carpet and scrambled onto his bed among the aged volumes. "Can you make some room? I'm never sleeping in a bed by myself ever again."

Still eyeing her in disbelief, he laid his book on the stand, pushed others aside, and pulled back the sheet and blanket. "Come on." He patted the empty space beside him. "I hope Mama doesn't appear in here."

"Yeah. I'm really hoping this is a bummer free zone." If she hadn't been majorly unglued, a thrill would've run through her at the glimpse of his bare thigh. It still kind of did.

He tugged his shirt down where the cloth had climbed up. "Pray excuse me."

"No biggie." It totally was. She crawled in beside him.

He closed strong arms around her, and she snuggled against his warmth, resting her head on his solid chest. Despite her being rattled like windows in a gale, his supreme hotness wasn't lost on her, or how physically close they finally were, or how to-the-core aware she was of his very essence. Of him.

An herbal scent pervaded the room above the spicy hint of his cologne. "Are you burning herbs, too?"

He pressed his lips to her head. "Why? Are you?"

"Someone was when I journeyed back in time. For the sick room, I guess. What have you got going on in here?" She pointed at the big multifaceted stone on his chest of drawers glinting in candlelight. "Is that a magic ball?"

"Large crystal. I burned sage earlier." He pointed at the herbal bundle on the mantel. "I have a bunch of angelica, dill, betony, and agrimony to guard against evil. And I hung rowan above the doorframe. You might know it as mountain ash."

She elbowed him reproachfully. "You didn't give me any?"

"I hung rowan over your door."

"Oh. I wondered what those twigs were for. They're shaped in small crosses and tied with red thread."

"Old Scottish tradition. I have some for our pockets. They're amulets from ages past."

"Where did you learn all this herbal stuff?"

"From Eloise at the shop."

Lorna tried to think which one she was. "That thin serious girl with glasses?"

"The very one. While you were rehearsing solos, I stopped at the shop for a scoop of lavender ice cream. Eloise said she sensed a darkness over me, like a thickening cloud."

Foreboding pricked Lorna. "Is she psychic or something?"

"Something," he affirmed. "Eloise also mentioned her concern for you."

"Oh. Great. Do I have the cloud thing, too?"

"She didn't elaborate."

Lorna sensed he'd left something unsaid. "Maybe

we should bring in an exorcist?"

"Any priest we invite to Harrison Hall might banish us along with the rest of the strange occupants."

Indignation flared inside her. "Why? We have every right to be here. This is our home."

A smile warmed his blue-gray eyes. "I am glad to hear you say that."

"I meant every word."

"I know." He lightly stroked his thumb over her cheek, eliciting tiny tingles. "Do not trouble yourself about Eloise. What have we to lose from her aid? She also gave me more crystals. Mr. Cable said to take what I liked. There and there." He nodded at the clear quartz stones shimmering on furnishings. "I tucked some in your wardrobe and on the top."

"Thanks." She dropped her gaze to the snowy sheen along the bottom of the green painted wall and followed a trail of mini-crystals. Familiar ones. "Did you seriously pour salt around your room?"

He lifted one shoulder and let it drop, brushing against her arm. His every move sent exquisite ripples through her.

"Eloise suggested salt might be helpful," he conceded. "I poured some beneath the windows and the wall in your chamber."

"Funny. I hadn't noticed. Probably too tired from all the singing and dancing workouts. Worse than being in the army."

"Not entirely." His tone had a cynical edge.

"Right. Sorry. What do I know of long marches and battle?"

He tightened his hold on her, in forgiveness of her blunder, she assumed. "You are not expected to know this."

"Thankfully." She sighed. "Listen, Hart. We're not warding off vampires and demons here. At least, I don't think we are. The demon part is questionable with Theo. Though I still can't quite see him as a murderer."

"You do not cross swords with him twice daily. Even so, I take your point. Perhaps he is more inclined with an accomplice."

Her deepest fear. "Even so, how will herbs and crystals help with the duel?"

Hart was quiet a moment. "Alter the past, you mean."

"Yes. Exactly."

"I do not know how much protection they lend." He tapped the pile of books at his side. "I thought these might help. Mr. Cable offered me the use of his library."

She scanned the vintage volumes. "Generous, as ever. What are you reading about?"

"Me."

"Oh. Like googling yourself the old-fashioned way."

He didn't falter at her terminology. Granted, he had some knowledge of computers and the internet now.

"While you slumber I peruse the past. Mine."

She studied the firm angle of his jaw. "Have you learned anything?"

"Not a great deal. I fall in the duel at Theo Archer's hand, as we have been told. Little description is given, except to say all those looking on were convinced I would prevail. Indeed, had already done so. One account declares Theo cheated. Others are not certain what took place. Lady Jane says Adelaide was persuaded Theo enacted the vile deed that led to my death, though he did not act alone."

The back of Lorna's neck prickled and the tiny hairs stood on end. "But she has no idea who his accomplice was?"

"Not that I can find. I made one interesting discovery."

She hardly dared to ask.

"My sister did not wed Lee Carter as I expected she would, given the understanding between them."

"Really? Who did she marry?"

The edges of Hart's mouth drew down. "The last man I would expect her to wed. Well, nearly the last. Eli Turner."

She startled. "Theo's cousin and second in the duel? You told me you don't trust this guy."

"Nor do I. He is hotheaded. Such impetuousness is dangerous."

"Wait a minute," she interjected. "We found nothing significant about Eli. Shouldn't our sources have said he wed Adelaide? Shouldn't Lady Jane have known he was her ancestor?"

"Yes. But she descends through their daughter and the name soon alters after the girl marries. Eli's full name is Samuel Elijah Turner. Some accounts list him only as Samuel. The recording may be confusing to his descendants."

"Not nearly as confusing as other stuff," Lorna muttered. "OK. Adelaide marries this dude you don't like. What happens to Lee Carter?"

"I have no notion. He disappears from the pages of history."

"How odd." She struggled to comprehend.

"Perhaps he was brokenhearted by your death and her refusal to have him and moved away."

"Perhaps. He was a dedicated dragoon. I cannot imagine him abandoning the cause. If so, I pity him." Hart was solemn.

"Yeah. Someone ought to have recorded what became of him."

"I agree." He met her insistence with a long pensive gaze. "Tomorrow is Midsummer Eve. With the house reawakened, we do not know what we may face."

"We know of my resolve to prevail no matter what. You shall live on here with me and Father John and our new friends. And, brace yourself," she cautioned. "My mother and sisters are coming to the performance and are eager to meet you. My father's away on business and cannot attend. They will take videos for him and you are spared that meeting for now."

He smiled faintly. "It will be no trial to meet your family."

"Say that after you actually have. Mom is kind of crazy, but nice, and the girls are, well, girls. All of them are eager to see some ghosts."

A chuckle escaped him. "Easily done, if they know how to look. What have you told them of me?"

"Oh, that you are my co-star and really cute."

His forehead creased. "Like a puppy?"

"No. Definitely in a manly way."

Humor flickered at his lips. "I am relieved to hear it, and that you have not described me as a dandy."

"Never that. I also told them I'm on my second lifetime, and we were an item in the first one. A couple," she amended. "But the eighteenth century wedding thing didn't work out."

He arched skeptical brows. "You did not share this?"

"No. A bit much for anyone to grasp. Even us."

"Yes." Somberness shadowed his eyes.

"I don't know where Theo thinks he is," she added.

"In the land of milk and honey," Hart summed up. "The younger son of a not wealthy gentlemen whose brother will inherit what little there is, dependent on the pleasure of his aunt and uncle, and cousin, Eli, now doted on by the extravagant Mr. Cable and Bill O'Neill."

"They're tickled to find him. He's perfect for the part."

"He *is* the part," Hart reminded her.

"Somehow, I tend to forget that. Theo's lack of an obvious killer instinct, I suppose."

"Dig deeper. He's after Adelaide's large dowry."

Lorna drew back. "You don't think he wants her for herself?"

"I honestly do not know if any of them do. Even Lee. And remember, with me out of the way, she inherits the entire estate upon my father's death. We have no younger brother to step in."

Too shocked to speak, Lorna pondered wordlessly.

Silence stretched between them, broken, at last, by Hart. "If…I do not live beyond tomorrow…"

Her heart lurched and she clapped her fingers to his mouth. "Stop right there. We tried living without each other once, and it didn't go well. If you hadn't gotten yourself fatally wounded in a duel you would have managed to fall nobly in some battle or the other."

He closed his hand around her fingers, easing them aside to speak. "Possibly. But you did not have to go on without me. I, alone, endured the pain. I cannot bear to think of you suffering as I did."

Neither could she.

"Promise me, you will be happy, Lorna. Come what may. Swear it." Emotion imbued his every word.

Dread weighed her middle. She determinedly cast it off. "No need for this vow. What shall come is that we will dance beautifully, give a brilliant performance, and then announce our engagement. You remember that part, right?"

Surprise sparked in his eyes. "Certainly. If…"

"Stop with the *ifs*," she hissed furiously. "I cannot. *Will not*. Go on without you. Get that through your thick head, and fight like you've never fought before and may never battle again to remain with me. And by heaven, I'll fight with you and for you. And God help anyone who gets in my way."

He gave a low whistle. "You could marshal troops into battle. I can envision you now, riding back and forth before the men. Only you do not ride."

"Pacing then, waving my hands and shouting. But there is only one man I want to marshal. And he had better take heed." Cupping her hands to Hart's cheeks, she brought his lips to hers in a kiss both tender and fierce.

He clasped her in his arms, returning the heated pressure on his mouth, kissing her harder than he ever had before…in this life or the last. Their fiery passion could ignite a blaze without matches. She burned deep into her most intimate self for him.

Was it only the song in her wildly beating heart or did music flow from the walls? Pulsing chords filled her very soul. They could soar together to another realm.

Hart rolled over with her down onto the bed. She breathlessly stripped off her t-shirt, and he tore off his shirt, muscles rippling in the soft glow. He held her to him, skin touching skin, his chest rising and lowering against hers in shallow pants. The hair on his chest was strange against her breasts but good. How divine he felt. How right.

"You are so beautiful, Lorna." His voice a husky whisper.

"So are you."

A slight chuckle, and his breath warmed her neck. He nuzzled her bare shoulder and tremors shimmered through her.

He slid his hands over her smooth back, and she sensed him grow more earnest. "My dearest darling. I may not be here this time tomorrow."

"You are here now." She covered his lips again, lengths of her hair slipping golden over his face. A tear coursed down her cheek and onto his. "We have waited over two hundred years to be together. Don't you think that's enough?"

"More than enough." He kissed up the tingly curve of her neck to her damp cheek. Lifting his head, he bent over her, his eyes deep gray-blue pools. Longing welled in their depths. "Let us make this night last if we must go two hundred more."

Chapter Sixteen

Midsummer Eve

The hour had come. The candelabra glittered overhead in the impressive foyer where Lorna and Hart were forming lines with the other couples in their troupe/cast. After rocketing into exploding stars with him in the night, and a hectic day of preparation—she thought Mrs. H. would never cease fussing over her costume—the big eve was upon them. Events were unfolding like a play. Granted, they were starring in one, and yet, this was infinitely more.

To further heighten tension, Mr. Cable had engaged a cameraman to film the opening dances and impending production. Given enough backing, he and Bob O'Neill were serious about making a dramatic indie musical romance. This was the trial run, and she must not screw it up for them.

The cast also had high hopes for their future, and she'd hate to let the other players down. Even Theo was strangely psyched about his role, and his *bad boy's* solo. Perhaps if she maintained a poised demeanor, neither the camera nor the audience would glimpse her quaking vulnerability.

As leading lady and vocalist, she bore an enormous weight on her slight shoulders. This production was a whole lot heavier to carry than the high school version of *Les Misérables* she'd starred in. Hart's burden was even greater. Her part ended before his. In essence, this was his story, though it was presented as both of theirs. Mr. Cable had tentatively entitled the production 'Harrison' not Randolph.

Battling to conceal palpating jitters behind a veneer of confidence, she lifted her eyes to Hart's. The heat in his smile melted her facade like the wax pooling in candles that glowed from every surface.

Whew. So much for projecting assurance. She could but hope the audience and potential supporters found her flutters engagingly adorable.

He clasped her hand in his steady grasp. 'You're ready,' he mouthed, shoring up her uncertainty.

She swallowed, and nodded.

Twangs from tuning instruments carried through the open windows and double doors. The string ensemble had been seated outside above them on the second story portico at the front of the house. An assistant to Mr. Cable was on the elevated porch with the ensemble to conduct the group for the introductory dances. Father John only relinquished partial control because he couldn't be in two places at once. He would direct every aspect of the performance, including the elegant minuet and a spritely country dance, to be performed during the play.

Grand in his black tuxedo, thinning hair slicked over his bald spot, he stepped to the microphone at the front of the entryway. Guests lined both sides of the roped off center, reserved for the dancers, and clustered at the far end, stretching into the hall. The overflow spilled onto the landing and the lawn. Folk gazed in through the wide doorway left open for the occasion.

This many attendees couldn't possibly fit inside the house. It was standing room only except for Lady Jane who had a seat of honor. Mr. Cable had particularly wanted to open this eventful evening in Harrison Hall, so cramping must be endured.

"Good evening," he boomed into the unneeded amplifier.

Radiating enthusiasm, he nodded at everyone, including those outdoors, and waved for quiet amid the animated response. "I speak for all of us at Harrison Hall when I welcome you to a festive gala of dancing and a romantic glimpse into our colonial past, one laced with tragedy that took place at this magnificent old home."

As if Lorna needed reminding.

"It is with the greatest pleasure that I introduce our marvelous debut stars portraying Lieutenant Hart Harrison and Miss Lorna Randolph. The latter even bears the name of her ancestor. So does our dashing officer, according to him. You have only to glimpse their ancestral portraits to witness the astonishing resemblance they bear to those who have gone before them."

An appreciative ripple ran through the crowd, interspersed with gasps and sighs from romantically inclined females.

Father John smiled and gestured for attention. "These stellar actors came to me like a gift and are supported by a wonderfully talented cast. Consult your programs, or soothsayers, for further information on each member. Some, like our lieutenant, and villain, remain intriguingly mysterious." Laughter and titters rose from the gathering. He chuckled at his wit.

"Enough introduction, let us begin."

Hearty applause followed, and he stepped back. Music flowed in through the open windows and doors, as if from the house itself. Lorna had certainly experienced this phenomena before. However, the ensemble accounted for the hauntingly beautiful melody, and the dance commenced. The song was the same she'd heard her first morning here, and the troupe were performing the identical steps in the exact spot where she'd initially seen Hart and his otherworldly companions.

Irony or fate? Either way, shivery chills scattered down her spine.

Guests attired in their finest modern day or eighteenth century fashion looked on. Cast members and additional reenactors were among those in period dress. And Mr. and Mrs. Dare. *Of course*. These devotees wouldn't miss it.

She and Hart nodded at the pair, who returned the polite acknowledgement, evidently pleased by the evening's festivities. No one else seemed aware of their partially vaporous presence. Other phantoms might well be in attendance.

Heaven only knew what Lorna's excited mother and sisters would pick up on their camcorder, electronic voice phenomena recorder, electromagnetic field reader, and the rest of their ghost detecting gear. The readings should be off the chart. She'd alerted her family to potential paranormal activity at Harrison Hall, and they'd come equipped like participants in an episode of *Ghost Hunters*. Slightly embarrassing.

At least, they weren't wearing thermal imaging goggles. *Yet*. They might wander the grounds in them after dark and had already asked Mr. Cable if they could return another evening when things had quieted down and the spirits would be more audible. The carryall backpack on sixteen-year-old Thora wasn't so noticeable, Lorna tried to tell herself, even though no one else in evening dress wore one.

To the girls' credit they didn't shout, 'Rock it, Lorna!' giving her thumbs up and high fiving the air when she circled past instead. And her mother refrained from hooting as if at a sport's event, with the occasional cheer.

Hart's lips twitched. Plainly, he liked them.

Good. If all went as planned, her crazy family would soon be his in-laws.

Foreboding cast a shadow. When did anything go as planned?

Pushing doubt aside, she savored the perfect evening. Light breezes kept the foyer from being too stuffy despite the crowd. The mild weather should gratify guests from this realm or the next. Alluring scents filled the soft air. Lavender, roses, and sweet mignonette blossoms scented the house in lavish displays much as they would have in centuries past.

Lorna focused on circling in her sumptuous blue gown, skirts swirling, the ornately embroidered gilt bodice winking in the light. She was back in the white-blonde wig, iridescent feathers waving, a tortoiseshell comb adorning the carefully arranged tresses. Several coiled lengths slipped artfully over her shoulders. Mrs. H. had her made-up and dressed like Virginia's premier eighteenth century lady, down to her floral shoes with pink bows.

Hart was splendid in his fitted uniform, rich brown

hair tied back with a black ribbon. He blithely stepped in polished black boots. Together, they wove in and out of the other couples in the cotillion. After countless hours of rehearsal, she emulated his effortless movements. How satisfying to match him turn-for-turn, dipping, and flowing together.

Theo and Deb Riviera, who played Adelaide, also took part in the performance. The sandy haired actor, Frank Smith, portraying Theo's cousin and second, Eli Turner, and Sam Brady as Hart's friend and second, Lee Carter, each had partners. Pride swelled in Lorna at the troupe's fluid elegance. Dancing was more than entertainment, social interaction, and an opportunity for romantic exchange through the ages. Done well, dance was an artistic masterpiece.

Undeniably, romance was also paramount. She and Hart revolved side-by-side, their gaze locked on each other. Willing herself to think only of this wondrous moment, she lost herself in his eyes, as blue as she'd ever seen them. He must be rapturously happy. *For now.*

The movement changed. She spun away from him and back again. They passed from couple to couple, then he closed one arm around her back and took her extended hand. They glided between the other pairs completing the same graceful maneuvers. All the while, she was aware of their onlookers and the camera rolling.

She caught Lady Jane's catlike gaze on her as she spiraled past. The elderly woman sat in regal splendor, diamonds sparkling at her throat and a tiara on her white head. Mr. Cable stood by her side, and Bill hovered nearby with his camera. They appeared well pleased. Everything seemed to be proceeding as desired.

But was it? Doubt pricked her. She completed the final step to thunderous applause, and a sense of wonder winged her spirits heavenward. The men in the troupe bowed, and ladies curtsied to their appreciative audience, changing directions to acknowledge all those cheering them on from outdoors.

Go me. She'd actually carried it off. They all had.

A second livelier dance followed with whirling, jigs, and promenades, leaving her breathless and the audience elated. Again, deafening applause arose. Whistles and cheers erupted. She gazed over faces creased in smiles, including her gyrating mother and siblings. Thora was texting like mad, probably posting her big sister on every social media site out there, including some that may have arisen since she'd immersed herself in the world of Harrison Hall. The two younger girls didn't have cell phones yet. Thank heavens.

The initial dances concluded, Mr. Cable proceeded to the microphone. He thanked everyone for their enthusiasm and invited them to take their seats beside the stage in preparation for the performance. "*After* the troupe has passed through," he emphasized. "And please help yourselves to the refreshments. Consider this a dinner theater of sorts. The production will commence after a twenty minute intermission."

A tent fluttering streamers and illuminated with small white lights was set up on the lawn. Tables inside it were laden with food and beverages of all sorts, and staff on hand to assist the guests. Waiters and waitresses in black and white uniforms bearing trays of finger foods and drinks would also serve during the interlude and unobtrusively as the play unfolded. Not only was it Midsummer Eve but Lady Jane's birthday. An enormous cake waited to be lit.

Cake cutting and fireworks were planned for ten o' clock, with dancing to follow inside the house and on the grounds. The ball didn't conclude until the witching hour. Midnight.

This wasn't the time for the cast to mix and mingle; that would come later. Dancers paired off, Lorna waving at her ecstatic family. Hart gave a friendly wave and took her arm. He assisted her down the steps and through the sea of guests.

The hungry gaze of female attendees locked on him as they walked over the path bordered by neat flower beds. Some men cast Lorna flattering glances, but wigs weren't as hot as they once were, and her gown not the turn-on it was in the eighteenth century. She couldn't expect to knock 'em dead with her Marie Antoinette impression, as she termed herself.

Oh well. Hart scorched her with his every look, and it was a beautiful evening.

Colorful blooms contrasted with shades of green. Sweet scents tinged with spicy herbs perfumed the air and trees shaded the lowering sun. A seat of honor was again reserved before the stage for Lady Jane.

Lord preserve her. The ultimate challenge was soon upon them. Lorna's chest thumped, and her throat was dry. She and Hart were among the first on stage with tender dialogue and a dance as the performance opened with their courtship before her untimely demise. Mr. Cable had even composed a lament for that tragic parting which comprised their duet.

He'd also heard the account of eighteenth century Lorna's appearance to Hart following her death, apparently passed down through the family, according to Lady Jane, and included that scene. Weirder still. Then the inspired composer had Hart, renewed by her visitation, sing of his resolve to nobly battle on in the revolution. Other dragoons/actors join in his song with a triumphant declaration of independence. Every patriot's breast would blaze with pride.

The skirmish that transpired on stage between the British and Continental soldiers/reenactors was difficult to orchestrate. Mr. Cable wanted to capture the essence of the pitched battles Hart took part in, with him shouting orders and gallantly leading his men on horseback. Horses were too much for the wooden platform, so he had the fearless leader charge on foot instead.

Hart had actually experienced all of this, with modifications by their zealous director, in his recent memory. Events were a little hazier for Lorna. She only distantly recalled her previous existence and had to take his word for her inspiring appearance after death. She held to what she knew of the past and the dictates of Mr. Cable.

What if she botched her lines, or missed a note? Her knees shook and her fingers trembled. She had to get a grip and prayed for the poise to act her part well and not squawk.

"Lorna," Hart summoned, breaking into her thoughts. He smiled reassuringly and bent his head near her ear. "You can do anything you set your mind to and your heart on."

This production encapsulated both. Why he wasn't

a wreck, she couldn't imagine. His very life might be at stake, on top of everything else, and that gnawed at her.

They joined others behind the large platform. Mr. Cable had a partition erected for privacy from spectators and screens for the cast during hasty costume changes. He was a stickler for modesty. Extra wardrobe and props hung from poles or were stowed in chests that could be pushed beneath the stage in the event of rain. He'd balked at having the entire production performed indoors.

The troupe sat on camp chairs, blotting their fingers, heated brows, and the backs of their necks on disposable towelettes and swigged from water bottles handed out by assistants. Energy bars were distributed. Anyone requiring a bathroom break could visit the discreet porta potty. The brick outbuilding maintained as a restroom for guests had quite an overflow.

Makeup was retouched as actors readied themselves. Mrs. H. patted Lorna's face with powder to absorb any shine, tucked the compact in her pocket, and lifted the parasol she twirled later in the play. "Adjusted as you requested." The secretive woman pulled the end of the handheld length, briefly revealing the blade hidden within.

Lorna was now more armed than Hart or anyone else realized. Solos weren't the only thing she'd practiced these past two weeks.

Chapter Seventeen

'Harrison' the Performance

Music soared on soulful wings into the perfect June evening and dancers swirled like silk. Lorna and Hart sang from their depths, sharing a stirring glimpse into the surging emotion between them. His grieving tribute to his lost love, and her parting aria, had the audience fishing for tissues. Villainous Theo charmed with his wit and good looks. Soldiers battling in the name of king and country, and those sacrificing all for liberty, clashed in long ago battles—or this past year, in Hart's experience. Scene by vivid scene, the play progressed to a crowd bent forward in their seats.

Buoyed by her success and that of her fellow actors, Lorna waited off stage in tremulous headiness. She descended from her exalted height with the sudden awareness the production was speeding past. Like parting mist making the formerly shrouded landscape visible, she realized the climactic duel was at hand. The choir had assembled in white robes for their solemn entrance around Hart's fallen form and Adelaide's weeping figure to voice his heavenly sendoff in a moving anthem composed by Mr. Cable. It gave her the creeps every time they rehearsed this scene. But she had to admit it was effective.

Mauve and pink washed with copper painted the

western sky. *Sunset*. The time the original duel was said to have happened. Stage lights came on, and she could scarcely breathe.

As before, Hart hurled insults at Theo. He flung defiance, and challenge ensued. Steel rang out as it had over two centuries ago in the metallic song of swords. White-knuckling her grip on the parasol, she followed each step and resounding clash. The two men wielding genuine blades drew wide-mouthed gasps from the audience.

Hart never enacted this scene the same way twice, making their high-strung director doubly edgy. Theo had requested a choreographed scene, and he hadn't even known what that term meant until Sam Brady explained it to him. Mr. Cable conferred with both fencers and had methodically detailed each move.

Hart obliged only to a point, arguing he was 'keeping the action fresh.' He was too vital to the production to fire for his rogue antics, and his opponent never suffered so much as a nick. Theo thrust, parried, stepped, and sprang with admirable skill. Still, Hart outdid him. Every single time.

Was he proving Theo couldn't possibly have prevailed by repeatedly demonstrating that he, not the boyish beauty, was the winner? Lorna surmised this is exactly what he was doing. It goaded Hart that he'd gone down in history as the loser, despite rumors of cheating. How else could he disprove them?

"That noble young man will fall this very hour," a male voice said near her ear.

"Such a pity," a female agreed. "Brave handsome fellow."

Chilled at their dire prediction, she turned, jerking

upon seeing the Dares. She hadn't noticed them beside her. "What?"

They turned far-sighted eyes on her. Mr. Dare nodded his partially transparent bewigged head at the duelists. "We saw Lieutenant Harrison betrayed before."

"You mean the first time?"

His bushy brow furrowed. "Indeed."

"We are come to warn you, lest it occur again." Mrs. Dare spoke through pale lips, her face increasingly indistinct.

Mr. Dare grew more vaporous by the instant. "We must return to the house, dear lady. Never outdoors after dark." His insubstantial form faded, his brown tricorn hat and walking stick the last to go.

"Wait." Lorna bent toward his hazy wife, the emeralds at her throat winking like cat's eyes in the mist. "Can you tell me who betrays Hart?"

"Beware the one he calls…" Whiteness enveloped the woman, and she disappeared with her husband. But the faint word 'friend' trailed after her.

Lorna stared at the place they'd been, her thoughts wheeling. Hart had said the Dares were dead by the time of the first duel. They truly must be regular attenders at this ball, because they had to have witnessed it then as ghosts.

They'd come to her for his sake. Good of them. But she still had questions. *Come back! Which friend?*

Wait—what's happening?

One moment, she sought the vanishing couple, and the next, the stage was gone. She stood in the crowd around the two combatants crossing blades on the lawn. A midnight blue twilight cloaked the sky. There were no stage lights. Torches in the chilly breeze burned here and there. This June evening was ten degrees cooler than its twenty seventeen counterpart.

Oh, right. She'd heard a mini-ice age existed during colonial America. A strange observation. She must act. Now.

Real Adelaide stepped into the Dare's place at her side. Uttering her friend's name in an urgent whisper, Lorna reached out and gripped her arm below the fluted lace sleeve.

The young woman swiveled toward her, her eyes widening. "Lorna? You came back."

She held a finger to her lips, leery of recognition from those who thought her dead. "I feared I might. We might."

"Yes." Adelaide fluttered her hand at Hart and Theo. "This is all wrong, isn't it?"

"Hart wins, yet still dies. Help me stop it from happening," she pleaded.

Adelaide's chest heaved in the tight bodice showing beneath the green cloak rustling around her shoulders. "How?"

"He's betrayed. Keep a sharp watch out."

The girl craned her neck, arching on her toes, to see past those taller than she, which was most everybody. "For whom?"

"I don't know. A friend of Hart's." It sounded lame.

"My brother claims many friends and acquaintances. And it grows darker by the moment. I shall fetch more light." She jerked up her skirts and sped away.

Lorna stayed as she was. Angling her head from

side-to-side, she sought their potential nemesis while continually returning to the fight. Did Hart realize the house had taken him back to the original encounter? Had Theo yet noted? Both were intent on the other.

They must know. Turf, not boards, lay beneath their feet, and no one looked on from seats. Their audience stood and all of them wore period dress. People strolling the grounds had collected around the sword-wielding men. Music floated from the house where many guests still supped and danced, unaware of events transpiring outdoors. Accounts said Hart's mother didn't learn her beloved son had fallen until afterward.

Somehow, Lorna must prevent the fatal wound. But how? She had no idea from whom it would come, or where, and wasn't entirely certain when. Her gut clamped as if in a vise and her heart raced. Despite the chill, her palms were sweaty.

"Lorna?" She inhaled sharply. Breathing in the acrid scent of torches and the sweetness of the white magnolias glowing in the tree nearest her, she spun around to find Sam Brady. His wig shone like a beacon in the graying light.

He gaped at their altered surroundings. "What in hell just happened?"

"We've traveled back in time. The house brought you, too. No idea why. I've journeyed back and forth several times."

He gestured at the encircled combatants. "You mean, this is the real deal?"

"Afraid so." Her mistrust of Sam had diminished over days of acting and dancing together, and she was desperate for an ally. "Hart and Theo are both from this era."

He blew out his breath. "That explains a lot."

"Yeah. I am, too, in a sense. Hart's in grave danger. We must discover who's about to strike him."

"Theo." Sam stated the obvious.

"I'm warned another's on the prowl." She scanned the faces cast in torchlight and pointed at a man on the perimeter of the duelists. "That's Eli Turner. Theo's cousin." He resembled Frank Smith, the tall sandy-haired actor who played him. One man in the knot of people behind Hart jogged her memory. He wasn't swarthy like Sam, but fair-haired like Theo, with a similar build. She singled him out. "There's Lee Carter."

"The real me, huh? Looks more like Theo." He waved a hand at his blue, red-faced uniform. "Why does Mr. Cable have me in this dragoon getup, if I could have worn a civilian suit? Real Lee's in a russet coat. Similar to Theo's—"

He broke off at Adelaide's breathless return. The girl hitched up her skirts with one hand, a torch raised in the other, dangerously near her hair. He grasped the base of the smoky light. "Here. Give me that before you catch yourself on fire." She released it to him, and he held it aloft.

"Don't shine it my way. I'm dead in this era," Lorna whispered. "He's with me," she explained to her stupefied friend. "No time for formal introductions. Adelaide meet Sam. He portrays Lee in our modern-day production."

She studied him, her lips parted. "You do not resemble my betrothed in the slightest."

Sam waved her aside impatiently. "We've already

covered that ground. The question is, if Theo made advances to you, why isn't this Lee's fight, instead of your brother's?"

Adelaide opened her mouth, but no words escaped her.

"My thoughts exactly," was his sardonic reply.

The ring of steel returned their focus to the duel. Hart made an astonishing leap, whipped around, and nicked Theo's arm through the sleeve with the tip of his blade, a variation of his actions in the play. Lorna assumed the deviation was for the expectations of this alternate reality, one with which his opponent was well-acquainted.

A cheer went up from their avid onlookers.

Hart held his sword in readiness. "Will a scratch suffice, or do you require a deeper wound as proof of my victory?"

"No. I accept." Theo lowered his blade and gave a curt bow. He sheathed his sword.

Hart did the same and slid his sword into its place at his side.

Clasping his bloodied arm, Theo turned away as they'd repeatedly rehearsed, then halted. The torchlight on his face revealed no joy in rejoining the past he'd left behind. He wore a 'now what?' expression.

Hart shifted his wary scrutiny at the surrounding ladies and gentlemen, attendees at his eighteenth century ball. He must wonder what the house was up to, unless…he knew.

Eli drew a handkerchief from his pocket and quickly bound Theo's minor injury. "You did well, cousin. Come. 'Tis over."

"Wait." Theo ran his searching gaze over the

collection. He lifted his hand to Sam and Lorna.

Sam returned the gesture. She didn't want to attract undo attention, when she no longer belonged in this era. Eli urged Theo away. Gone, the swaggering villain he'd portrayed.

"Poor bastard," Sam muttered. "Back to God knows what kind of life."

"Yeah." She pitied him. "We must focus on Hart."

Lee clapped his fellow officer on the shoulder. "Well done, Lieutenant. As always. I would expect nothing less of you. Is that not right, folks?"

Applause and cheers answered. Hart bowed and nodded to show his appreciation. Men in civilian dress and uniforms stepped forward to shake his hand. His tribute done, Lee strode into the murkiness among the trees lit only in places where twisting torchlight fell.

"Why doesn't he invite his good friend to join him in a celebratory drink, or come in search of his dear betrothed? After all, this duel was fought over her," Sam observed.

"Excellent questions." Adelaide snatched up her skirts and darted through the assembly like a tenacious dog. Small breeds were the fiercest. Hart embraced his sister and bent his head near hers. They spoke together as he'd done in the play.

"Eerily familiar," Lorna whispered to Sam. "What are we to do now?"

"Watch."

"Easier said than done." Between the sooty smoke, gawping onlookers, and deepening gloom, it was difficult to clearly see Hart. "Is Adelaide warning him, do you think?"

"Hard to say. There's discussion between them and

shaking of heads." Sam pointed. "Look. There. At Hart's rear."

She strained to see past the throng to the figure muted by shadows. His fair hair stood out. "Suspicious."

"If what you say is true, very." The torch in hand, Sam started toward the potential menace.

A sense of urgency seized Lorna, and she fought to push past bystanders. "Make way!"

"Look where you're treading," a woman berated her.

The inebriated hulk barring her path refused to budge. "Get out of here," he grunted, reeking of rum.

Sam sent him reeling. "Step aside for the lady."

"Thanks." But it was like swimming upstream. More onlookers closed in. People she'd swear hadn't been there a few moments before appeared. And they chatted loudly, making it nearly impossible to converse below a shout.

Why were they still hanging out on the lawn, anyway? The duel was over. It was if these antagonists blocked her on purpose. Was the house conspiring against them?

Screw it. "Nothing to see here!" She shoved at bodies like a bratty teen fighting for tickets to see her favorite performer, not the lady she resembled. Making little headway.

Where were they all coming from? Why had Adelaide made it through the blockade and not her? Should she call out to Hart?

Anyone who recognized her would freak. He knew his dire history. Surely, his *Spidey senses* were fully tuned in?

"Sam, what's happening?" He had the advantage in height.

"Not sure. The dude stepped away. No. He's back. Wearing a russet coat. Could be Theo or Lee. Or anyone. I can't see—"

A terrible premonition came over Lorna. "Hart!" Her desperate shout coincided with the agonizing cry that rent the night and sliced her to the marrow. "Oh, God. No."

"Damn. Come on. I have training as a medic." Sam waved his torch menacingly. "Move!"

Forgetting everything except getting to Hart, she raced behind him through the sea of people tightening around what she feared was his fallen form with his sister sobbing at his side. Adelaide's cries were audible now.

Why hadn't she and Sam been quicker? Why had they continually been thwarted from getting through?

"Theo!" Adelaide hurled the nearly incoherent charge at the supposed culprit.

Had he dared, even now? Eli led him away. Had he returned? Was it his fair head they'd spotted, and his coat?

Questions churning amid searing anguish, she burst into the inner circle. The bewildered young man stood staring at the bloody knife in his hand as if he had no idea how it came to be there. She knew for a fact Theo didn't have it on him when the house brought them back. Only his sword. Mrs. H. hadn't yet given him the prop knife, and it sure as hell didn't resemble this stained dagger.

Hart writhed on the ground, his face twisted in pain. Adelaide's was contorted between despair and rage. Thank God the blow wasn't instantly fatal as portrayed in the play. Life meant hope, Lorna reminded herself, between ragged breaths and the stark terror that threatened to tear her apart.

Sam pushed his way through the throng like a bouncer. "Take this." He shifted the torch to a gaping gentleman. "Hold it so I can see what I'm doing." He dropped to his knees beside Hart, and gently turned him, groaning, onto his side. The ugly gash bled profusely. "We've got to stop the flow." He undid Hart's long white cravat, wadded it, and pressed the improvised bandage to the wound. "Keep it in place," he instructed Adelaide, who held out trembling fingers. He unknotted his own neck cloth, wrapped the length around Hart's front and back to secure the pad, and bound the ends. This swift action took seconds.

He slid an arm beneath Hart's head. "You have internal injuries, buddy. A possible laceration to the liver, punctured ribs. I can't say what for certain. Surgery is imperative."

Fury mixed with the desperation engulfing Lorna. Should they get Hart into the house and the portal? That would cost precious time. And where was the perpetrator of this vile deed? Rumblings in the crowd were laced with the name *Theo*.

He threw down the knife. "I didn't bloody do it!"

Fingers pointed. "The evidence is at your feet."

"No. This is not my blade. Carter stuck it in my hand."

A familiar face caught her eye on the outskirts of the angry assembly. Lee Carter. Why hadn't he rushed to Hart's side at once? He'd acted peculiar this entire evening. Maybe he did frame Theo.

"Hart's still alive?" He sprinted at the tight cluster around the wounded man, as if it suddenly occurred to him. "You! Send for a doctor!" he shouted at Sam. "My dear friend. My poor sweet Adelaide."

Actor. Nothing in his declaration rang true, and he was attempting to rob them of the one man with life-saving medical skills.

Lorna reached Hart before he did and squeezed in with Adelaide and Sam. "I'm here." Forcing herself to be calm for Hart's sake, she fought inner turmoil and knelt beside him, stroking his hair and pale face. "Hold on. Help is coming."

He fluttered his eyes at her, grimacing. "Up to you now, sweetheart. *Justice*," he ground out between gritted teeth.

What he wanted most, next to a second shot at a life with her. Why couldn't he have both?

"Stay with him, Sam. No matter what. We're getting him home. But first—" She sprang to her feet, pulled the sword secreted in the length of her parasol, and rounded on Lee in a whirl of skirts. She held the tip to his throat. "You did this. Come to finish the job, have you?"

"Lorna?" He gaped at her. "You're dead. I attended your funeral."

"It didn't take. Drop your sword, traitor."

He arched away from her, waving his arms at the goggling bystanders. "She's mad. Must have escaped from an asylum. They faked her death."

"Oh, I died. I'm back." She drew blood from the prick at his neck. "Your turn to give it a go. Drop it."

"She will dismember you, man," Sam assured him.

He sullenly undid his sword belt, and it fell to the

188

ground. "On your knees," Lorna hissed.

Adelaide screeched to life. "No! Lee wouldn't do this."

Lorna had no such illusions. "Would and did. And left Theo holding the blade belonging to him. Look at the carving on the handle." She remembered the distinct knife from the dim recesses of her past. Who else had a snake carved on the handle with glittering ruby eyes? Positively medieval, probably used in some ritual involving human sacrifice.

Eli joined his dazed cousin, possibly drawn by Adelaide's shrieks and sobs. He picked up the dagger and examined the ornate inlay. "Aye. 'Tis Carter's."

Lee cast a scornful gaze at Eli. "I had not yet marked its absence. The knife is worth a fortune. Your disreputable cousin stole it from me. A would-be murderer and a thief."

Blue eyes blazing, Eli pointed the knife at its owner. "You dare blame this fiendish act on him? Scoundrel!"

That made two of them with blades to his throat.

Angry men circled Lee. "Saw you skulking in the trees," one said.

He stabbed his finger at Theo. "Could have been him. What's he doing here now, huh? Ask yourselves that."

"I returned for my friends," Theo attempted.

"You have none," Lee scoffed.

"He has me," Sam growled. "We've no time for this, folks. We must get Lieutenant Harrison proper medical attention."

Terror ratcheted through Lorna. She fixed her devastated gaze on Hart. "Why, Lee?" the faint query escaped him, then his eyes fluttered shut.

"We're losing him." Sam immediately began pushing on his chest in a fight for his life. "Adelaide, cover him with your cloak. Better than nothing."

She tucked the green taffeta around her brother, tears streaming down her face. Then she scrambled to her feet and hurtled herself at Lee. "You've killed him!"

Eli flung an arm around her waist to restrain her. He pulled her back and stepped between the enraged young woman and her fiancé, now target. "Let me tend to him, sweet lady. I shall see justice done."

Rude fingers stabbed at Lorna from the multitude. "What of her? Has she bewitched Carter into doing her bidding?"

"What? No. I love Hart. I'm only here for his sake."

"From your grave, witch? We saw your coffin lowered." Accusations hurled at her and rough hands reached out.

Images of the flames burned in her mind. Not only fear for herself, but terror for Hart flooded her like a stream pouring over its banks and washing out everything. He might still be revived. How could she help him if they imprisoned her?

"Is the sister in on this? Inherits all, doesn't she, if her brother dies?" Fresh outcries added fuel to the rapidly increasing inferno.

Dear God. They were fast losing their minds. Those who had begun the evening as dignified guests at the ball were spiraling into mob mentality.

Eli threatened anyone snatching at Adelaide with the knife. "Not another word against Miss Harrison or I will cut out your lying tongues."

Lorna had no doubt he meant it. There was a steel about him. She remained close to Hart, fending off attackers with her sword. Anyone coming too near her got a bloody swipe. Feral howls rose. But she couldn't defeat them all, and Eli must defend Adelaide. He snatched up Lee's sword, giving him a second weapon. He didn't have his own blade on him. Not every gentleman considered them mandatory accessories for a ball.

All the while, Lee watched with smug satisfaction. Did he truly think the heinous deed would be pinned on the women? She'd slash his pompous face and demand to know why he'd committed this outrage against a friend.

"Stop!" Adelaide screamed. "Miss Randolph is as innocent as I am."

"Why's she here then? 'Tisn't natural," a woman called.

"She has returned to us like an angel."

Hissing greeted this assertion. "A devil, more like." The buzzing swarm closed in.

"Allow me, Lorna." Theo exhibited his former control.

Should she trust him? He was by far the better swordsman. She made a split-second decision. "Give this to Adelaide." She passed her sword to him, and he conveyed it to the fiery girl.

Theo then positioned himself between her and the salivating pack. A few well aimed thrusts, angry bellows, and they backed off to lick their wounds. They'd think twice about taking him on again. Meanwhile, inexorable seconds ticked by, vital moments draining Hart's life.

"If you know the way, Lorna, I strongly suggest you get us out of here," Theo said over his shoulder.

They couldn't possibly penetrate the ravening mob acting like zombies, even if Hart could be moved. The compact portal wouldn't hold him, her, and Sam. She should aid the maligned Theo, and what about Adelaide? She gazed at her friend.

She waved the sword at her. "Go, if you are able to, Lorna. We will be all right." She narrowed eyes so much like her brother's at Lee. "He has a reckoning coming."

"I do not know how or where you intend to depart. But I swear I shall see to Miss Harrison and that culprit," Eli vowed. "I'm every bit the swordsman he is. Better. I hereby challenge Lee Carter to a duel, and it won't be to first blood."

She gave a nod. "I should like to see that, but we must go. Immediately."

Their only hope lay in the house hearing her. It had responded to her before. Perhaps it would again.

She knelt on the ground and cradled Hart's head in her lap, her arms around his shoulders. "Hold on, baby." Closing her eyes, she channeled all her heartfelt determination into one supreme directive. "Take us back! Now!" she shouted at the unseen entity.

A quick spiral. Blinking in the stage lights, she found herself on the platform still holding Hart while Sam performed chest compressions. Theo guarded them with his sword. "Ambushed!" he cried.

"Call 911!" Sam directed. "Get blankets. Hart's gone into shock. Anyone know his blood type? He'll need a transfusion."

A flurry of activity blurred before Lorna. The audience huddled in their seats, too shaken to move. Horror etched her mother and sister's faces. Cast members fell over each other getting blankets and calling an ambulance. She'd gotten Hart back alive. Barely. The house had obliged.

Mr. Cable's alarmed gaze swam into view. He bent near the tight group around the wounded star. "How could this happen? The blade struck him out of nowhere. All we saw was an arm wielding a knife behind him. No idea who it belonged to."

That must have been how the attack appeared to them, and time was compressed, so they'd missed what followed in the past. It must seem like seconds to onlookers here.

"I have men searching the grounds for the culprit," he added shakily.

Lady Jane stood at her nephew's elbow with Bill O'Neill's support. She leaned on her gold-top cane. "My poor girl."

Lorna was almost too overcome to speak. "We know who stabbed Hart. Lee Carter. The *real* Lee. It's always been him."

Mr. Cable peered at her through his glasses like a baffled owl, and Bill stared as if not truly seeing.

Sirens sounded and lights flashed in the distance. "Don't you boys understand?" Lady Jane asked in her soft voice. "Hart and Theo are *originals*. And Lorna has lived here before, as the young lady she plays. The house brought them together."

Insight penetrated the men's blank expressions. "Good Lord," murmured Father John.

Bill clapped a hand to his head. "I've been so

dense."

Lorna returned her questing gaze to the wise woman. "Why? How has this all happened?"

"You, dear girl. Your love for Hart went into the very fiber of this house when you died, as did his for you. Harrison Hall absorbed your heart's desire. A powerful essence combined with the paranormal force already at work here. Love is the greatest magic of all."

Tears slid over her cheeks. "What good will it do if he doesn't live?" She gazed down at him through the liquid film. How pale and still he was.

Lady Jane laid a sympathetic hand on her head. "The past cannot be undone, child. He died there. Thanks to Sam, he may live anew."

Sam huffed from his exertions. "He isn't gone yet."

She squeezed Hart's cool fingers. "I'm here with you. Don't you dare leave me. Keep fighting. Harder than you fought the British, harder than you've fought for anything or anyone before. You fight for me, Hart Harrison. For us."

Sniffing, she swiped at her eyes with her sleeve. "We will be together. I promise. Don't ever let go of that hope. Battle on, you hear me? Don't give up."

He fluttered his eyes at her, as if he really saw, then shut them again.

Lady Jane passed her a tissue. She mopped her face, then pressed her lips to his forehead. "Live, my darling." Her voice cracked and if Lee hadn't been doing chest compressions, she would have thrown herself on Hart.

Lights flashed on the red and white emergency vehicle parked as near to the stage as possible. She clung to Hart, but Mr. Cable pulled her away. "You've done your work, now let them do theirs."

"Can we ride in back with him?" she choked out.

"I'll drive you—"

"You're badly shaken, John," Bill gently broke in. "I will drive you and Lorna and anyone else who fits in my car."

"I'm coming." Sam moved aside for the man in a green uniform carrying a bag. Two other medical workers hoisted a stretcher.

"Me, too." Theo appeared truly grieved.

Lorna wanted to scream to God, the house, the universe.

Let him live!

Chapter Eighteen

Ceaseless prayer on her lips, the smell of sanitizer in her nostrils, Lorna sagged between Mr. Cable and Bill on the cushioned bench. The intensive care waiting room was empty of everyone now except for their small party. She'd had no opportunity to change her gown before piling into the car for the hasty ride here, but had ditched the wig and exchanged her eighteenth century shoes for sandals. The men were in shirt sleeves, their tuxedo jackets draped over chairs. Sam and Theo, also in costume, minus Sam's wig, idly worked on the jigsaw puzzle spread over the table in the center of the room.

How many distraught people had put that together in the past weeks, or months?

Not her mom, who actually liked piecing puzzles. After a lot of hugs, the deeply sympathetic woman had taken the girls home with Lorna's promise to keep them posted. Shocked cast members awaited texts and calls after a nurse had urged them on their way. The stricken audience must watch the news for updates. Mrs. H. had reluctantly remained behind to oversee things at Harrison Hall and anxiously awaited reports.

How long had it been now? Three hours? Four? The hands on the white-faced wall clock were agonizingly slow. Was Hart still in the operating room? No medical personnel had informed them differently.

Surgeons were repairing the damage to his liver and whatever else they'd found, and replenishing his blood. He'd lost a lot. Cast members had donated blood to replace the units he'd needed, and because the hospital had an ongoing blood drive. Weirdly, Hart and Theo were the same type. The former villain had his minor wound properly bandaged while he was at it. Only the crimson tear in his shirt showed where Hart had scratched him during the duel.

The sight of it brought everything flooding back. The clash of blades, the vile dagger, betrayal, and deceit. Also, the rush of aid that came to her and Hart for which she was eternally grateful. *Dear God, let it matter*. Small comfort if he breathed his last in the present rather than the past.

Father John circled a comforting arm around her shoulders. "Hart will be all right. You got him to us in the nick of time."

She fought to control the quaver in her voice. "*Touch and go*, the doctor said."

"That was at first," he reminded her. "The last report was better."

She leaned into his kind embrace. "I know. But I won't believe he's all right until I see for myself."

"You look utterly exhausted, Lorna. Try and close your eyes for a few minutes."

"Or take up drinking a lot of coffee," Bill interjected. "Anybody else want some?"

Mr. Cable raised his hand.

"Of course." Bill smiled faintly, going in search of a fresh cup for them both.

She couldn't stomach coffee. Her churning gut barely tolerated the gingery soda. The guys each had a can or two of their preferred beverage, given the selection. Theo probably would have opted for ale.

Sam glanced up from the puzzle, appearing quite different with his spiked black hair. Put him in a modern-day suit and he'd make a suave *maître d'* for a swanky restaurant. He also kind of resembled a hit man. "Hand the girl a sword. She'll come to life. And God help any man who gets in her way."

A faint smile tugged at Theo's lips. "She left her blade a few centuries back with Adelaide. I hope she finishes Lee off with it."

"That would be something." A speculative expression came into Sam's ebony-colored eyes. "Say, I wonder if we changed history?" He reached for his phone.

Given the unusual circumstances of their seventeen seventy-seven visit to Harrison Hall, they hadn't divulged the details of Hart's injury to everyone. But word had spread through the cast regarding *the strange paranormal event* and would spread farther. Mr. Cable might as well organize ghost tours. He'd be besieged.

"Anyone got a signal? My battery's dead." Sam pocketed his useless phone.

"I'll check." Mr. Cable lowered his arm from Lorna and reached into his pants pocket. He took out his phone. "Yep. I do. I'll see what I can find on Hart Harrison," he said, scrolling with buffed fingernails.

The manicure had been for the production. How long ago that seemed now. Hart, vibrant and strong, now lay on an operating table clinging to life. She prayed he'd hold on for all he was worth. *More.* For both of them.

"Listen to this." Father John paused, scanning the

text on his phone. "It mentions the duel, and that Hart was stabbed in the back by a former friend, Sergeant Lee Carter. That's new information."

A hint of satisfaction crossed Theo's gaze. "Did the duel between Eli and Lee take place? Or did Adelaide get him?"

Eyes widening behind his glasses, Mr. Cable nodded. "Wow. Not the sister. Eli ran him through."

Theo applauded. "Well done, cousin."

Cheering might seem out of place in the waiting room. In this case, it wasn't.

Sam tipped his hand to their advocate. "To Eli, for justice done."

"Amen," Lorna added. "I'll bet Adelaide had his back."

Theo nodded. "No doubt, she did."

Mr. Cable grew more animated. "Listen to this. They found out Lee was a British spy."

"Really?" She pushed back tousled lengths of blonde hair. "I didn't see that one coming."

"They had secret spy rings during the war," Mr. Cable reminded her. "Some were quite famous."

"Yeah, but not to us. And Lee?" She shook her head, unable to grasp the truth.

"You think you know a guy," Sam said drily.

Theo wore his baffled look. "I actually did know him and never expected this."

"So did I. Once. A very long time ago." She fingered the lace at her sleeve, possibly quite an old habit. "He wore two faces."

"Those are the kind who make the best spies." Sam locked a puzzle piece into place. Theo had lost interest.

"The best spies are the worst sorts of traitors." She

nudged Mr. Cable, still avidly reading. "What else?"

"As smart as he was, Lee feared Hart would find out he was carrying messages. That accounts for the furtive attack. Plus, he'd get more money marrying Adelaide if she inherited the family estate."

"What a jerk," Sam muttered.

"Totally." She shifted in her full skirts, wishing she'd had time to change. The cloth poofed around her. "How did they discover all of this about Lee? Did he keep a girlie diary?"

"No. Letters were found among his things. Hart's duel with Theo was likely an opportune moment for Lee to carry out his murderous aim. He'd have found another way without it." Mr. Cable smoothed his mustache and his thinning hair. "There's more. Stories circulated that Hart's former love Lorna Randolph returned from her grave to intervene for him like an avenging angel. Some said a witch. And that he vanished with her into thin air. But these accounts are considered rumor."

She squirmed with an uneasy rustle. "So I should hope. We don't need more wild stories to deal with than we already have. Imagine the hordes of supernatural seeking freaks descending on the house."

He brushed aside her concern. "Don't worry about it. Few believe accounts too farfetched for their understanding."

"True. Some people don't believe their own eyes." She hadn't at first. "Does Adelaide still marry Eli?"

"Yes." Father John smiled at Theo. "It says you disappeared along with the others, but are no longer the bad guy in the tale."

His pretty face radiated gratification at these

tidings.

Sam high-fived him. "We did alter history."

"You surely did." Mr. Cable scanned more text. "This should make Hart's day when he wakes up. He was considered a promising dragoon, lauded for his wits and courage, and declared among the finest swordsmen of his day."

"Yeah, that will make him happy," Lorna agreed, even though the dread that he might not wake up constantly gnawed at her. The first phase of their mission was accomplished. He must live to fulfill the second.

The door opened, and the surgeon entered in blue scrubs. She went rigid, searching the mature man's thin face for clues in his chiseled brow, and the lines around his eyes and mouth. Either his expression was always mild, or he had nothing grievous to impart. She slowly exhaled.

Terms like, *in recovery… endured the procedure well… cautiously optimistic… strong young man… athleticism in his favor… antibiotics to ward off infection…*whirled around her in a hopeful swirl. Promising to send the nurse with more news soon, the doctor hurried away.

"Give the man a medal." Mr. Cable smiled encouragingly. "That's more like it. See? Hart's coming along."

She clung to every buoyant word lifting her above the dark fear that threatened to drag her under like an evil tide. When this was all over, she was going to sob hysterically, but not now. She had to keep it together.

How long she sat on the edge of her seat, she couldn't say. Entreaties to rest fell on deaf ears. She must be ready to charge out that door the second the go-ahead was given.

Finally, the anxiously watched exit opened, and a nurse entered in a blue and white uniform. Her glance took in the costumed visitors. "Lorna Randolph and Mr. John Cable?"

She sprang up, nearly falling over her skirts and sprawling on the floor in her haste. Mr. Cable steadied her and stood at her side. The others rose, including Bill, who'd long returned by this point.

The mature woman gestured them back. "Only two visitors at first. Mr. Harrison's adopted father and his fiancé."

Granted, Lorna was exhausted, but she didn't recall them making an announcement. "Me?" she nearly stuttered.

Impassive eyes considered her from behind wire-rimmed glasses. "If you are Lorna Randolph?"

"I am. He asked for me?" A spark of hope kindled.

She inclined her graying head. "We explained he can only see his nearest relatives, and he requested Father John and his fiancé."

Clever. How Hart had the presence of mind to pull this off after nearly dying and going through surgery, she didn't know.

"That's us," Mr. Cable assured the nurse, and they followed the assured figure.

Lorna would have gone with the nurse anywhere, even the bowels of Hell, if it led to Hart. But she preferred the hospital. She was vaguely aware of entering and exiting an elevator, a labyrinth of halls, and passing the nurse's desk with screens and lights on. She grew alert after they were directed to the sectioned off corner where Hart lay on a narrow hospital bed with metal railings on either side. He wasn't likely to hurl himself onto the tile floor, but she supposed they had to take precautions, and there were bound to be lots of rules.

Thank God. He had more color in his face than the last time she'd seen him, limp and pale in her lap. Despite the white wrappings around his middle, the IV tube in his arm, and other monitors, he still looked like Hart. The spark inside her grew into a flame.

"Hey," she said softly. "Lazing about, huh?"

He smiled weakly.

Battling the urge to curl at his side, she bent over and kissed his forehead, then pulled a chair as closely as possible to him and sank into it. For a long moment, she drank him in. Even the sanitized scent couldn't erase his essence. "You made it through."

"With a little help." His eyes were the same blue-gray as before. "I've been worse."

"You've been dead," she agreed. "But not this go round. You realize your grave is empty?"

"I hadn't thought of that."

"I've had plenty of time to think."

"Guess so." He gave her a sympathetic look, then shifted his focus to Mr. Cable. "I assume you are aware of *everything*?"

"Not sure if I've taken it all in yet, but I know who you and Lorna truly are. An indescribably remarkable story. Believe me, if I could convey it, I would."

Hart sipped the juice they'd brought him through a straw. "Will you star us in another play?"

"You can bet on it. But..." He was thoughtful. "What with the duel and the paranormal element in the house, I'm not sure it's wise to revisit your earlier era again."

"Maybe not." Hart's gravity reflected her solemn contemplation.

An inherent warning tolled inside her. "I hate for you to lose all the effort and money you put into that production, Father John. But it's too dangerous to risk being swept back there." She shuddered. "No point in tempting fate."

"None at all. Don't worry about me. Plenty of other opportunities to pursue." He breezed ahead. "I'm thinking of setting up a Shakespeare troupe, and doing *The Taming of the Shrew*, the musical. I'll compose the songs, of course. We can keep the cast we have. You two are my stars. And Theo, Sam…" He brightened, his thoughts flowing.

She eyed him in bemusement. "You planned all of this while we were in the waiting room, not knowing if Hart would live or die?"

"Oh, I always knew he'd live. The house didn't take you back and forth and give you this second chance for nothing. Like Aunt Jane said, there's no force as powerful as love."

"The greatest magic of all." Hart's voice was a whisper.

She considered him in wonder. "You heard? How? You were unconscious. I mean, there was a moment when I thought you might have."

"Oh, I heard a great deal." His eyes shone with the tears he winked back. "You fighting for me, and urging me to battle. Sam, Theo, and Eli taking my part. I lost one friend but gained new ones."

She covered his hand with hers, relieved to find his

fingers warmer. "Lee was a British spy. We read it on the internet. Did you never suspect?"

He exhaled slowly and groaned under his breath. "No. And yes. I see the signs now."

"Lee feared you would." She squeezed his fingers. "Enough about that traitor. When did we get engaged?"

He laughed, grimacing at the movement and resultant pain it caused him. "Between us? Several centuries ago. Officially? We have yet to make the announcement."

Mr. Cable brought his hands together. "Mend, Hart Harrison. I'm hosting an engagement party for my adopted son, which I shall make official, by the way, as soon as you get out of the hospital. Harrison Hall awaits your return."

"And likely the Dares with it. Big fans of yours." She had much to tell him when he was stronger— "Hold on. I'm a little spacey right now. Did you say you're adopting Hart?"

"Certainly. He can retain his own name, and there are some details to tend to like gaining documentation for him, and Theo, come to think of it. Neither of them have records." He tugged the lobe of an oversized ear, his pensive expression a reflection of the wheels whirring in his gifted mind. "No matter. I'll see to it. I've got connections and means. But back to Hart. By rights, Harrison Hall already belongs to him. I shall make certain it becomes his legal inheritance."

Hart seemed too overcome to speak. Lorna sat like a stunned statue.

"Thank you, sir," he managed, huskily. "I haven't the words to express my gratitude."

"You don't need them. I understand."

He and his soon-to-be adoptive father exchanged meaningful glances, and Mr. Cable patted his shoulder. "You'll have the wedding there, of course," he continued happily. "Bill loves to organize these sorts of things, and Mrs. Hill will fuss over every detail like an old hen. I wonder if you should get married before or after our next production, or hey, during? There's a wedding scene in *Taming of the Shrew…*"

While the eccentrically brilliant man dreamed aloud, she held Hart's hand, exploring his face. He never took his gaze off her. "You promised we would be together, and here we are," he reminded her.

"That was Lorna number one. Lorna number two just bungled into it, never quite knowing what she was doing. But she loves you with all her heart. That's one thing we have in common."

His eyes glistened. "It was you, dearest. When you urged me on as I lay with my head in your lap, it was just as you had the first time."

She cocked her head at him. "What do you mean?"

"I thought I lay in my bedroll in the tent when you appeared before and cradled me in your arms. But the words, the emotion, were the same. Identical."

Tiny chills scattered through her to her knees. "Everything?"

He nodded. "You even wore the same gown. I had forgotten the exact fabric. Only that it was you, and you were real."

"Did you flash forward to your near death in the future?"

"I think maybe so. You kept me going in the past, and tonight. I dreamed we were waltzing in the garden, circling through the hedges."

"Oh." Her voice caught. "When you were fading, earlier?"

His eyes spoke for him.

Shadowed figures danced in her mind. "Don't ever go there without me again."

He intertwined his fingers with hers. "No. Next time, we go together."

She tilted her head at Mr. Cable. "We want to waltz in the garden, if you could compose something for us. And we'll need the ensemble," she said, past the lump in her throat.

He surveyed them from behind his glasses. "Done. How about for your engagement party?"

"Perfect." Lorna could imagine it now, and judging from Hart's gaze, so could he.

"We shall be back in the garden where we first began, my lady. That is where I proposed."

Goosebumps scattered over her. The misting centuries cleared, and she heard his voice in her ear as if it were yesterday. "I remember."

A word from the author...

Married to my high school sweetheart, I live on a farm in the Shenandoah Valley of Virginia with my human family and furbabies. An avid gardener, my love of herbs and heirloom plants figures into my work. The rich history of Virginia, the Native Americans, and the people who journeyed here from far beyond her borders are at the heart of my inspiration. I'm especially drawn to colonial America and the drama of the American Revolution. In addition to historical romance, I also write time travel, paranormal, YA/NA fantasy romance, and nonfiction.

https://bethtrissel.wordpress.com/

Thank you for purchasing
this publication of The Wild Rose Press, Inc.

If you enjoyed the story, we would appreciate your
letting others know by leaving a review.

For other wonderful stories,
please visit our on-line bookstore at
www.thewildrosepress.com.

For questions or more information
contact us at
info@thewildrosepress.com.

The Wild Rose Press, Inc.
www.thewildrosepress.com

Stay current with The Wild Rose Press, Inc.

Like us on Facebook

https://www.facebook.com/TheWildRosePress

And Follow us on Twitter
https://twitter.com/WildRosePress